NATALIE MICHAELS

THE BONE FOREST

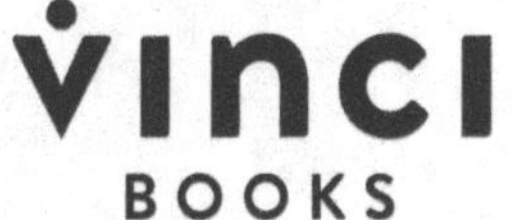

By Natalie Michaels

Steve Campbell Psychological Suspense Thrillers

The Last Girl

The Bone Forest

The White Dahlia

Vinci Books

vinci-books.com

Published by Vinci Books Ltd in 2025

1

A CIP catalogue record for this book is available from the British Library.
Paperback ISBN: 9781036705190

Chapter One

DON'T TRUST THE DEVIL EVEN THOUGH YOU KNOW HIM

The Dominant

Melissa closed her eyes as she succumbed to the pleasures her dominant was inflicting on her.

"What's your color?" he asked in a deep tone.

"Green," she said breathlessly.

"Do you want me to do it again?" he asked, this time with his lips close to her ear so he could watch all the hairs on the back of her neck and shoulders stand on end.

"Yes, please, Sir," she whimpered, licking dry lips.

The dominant leaned forward, kissed her left shoulder, then walked around her where he checked the leather restraints securing her wrists and ankles to the St. Andrew's cross; they were tight but not enough to stop blood flow.

Grabbing the crop from the hook on the wall, the dominant slapped it into his hand, creating a sharp snap sound, making his submissive flinch. His hand stung, but it wasn't hard; it had more sound than bite, so he knew it wouldn't cause harm.

He returned to Melissa and administered soft taps across her shoulder blades and then buttocks, each getting successively harder until leaving red welts across her soft, pink flesh. With each slap of the crop against her skin, Melissa cried out in pleasurable moans, which pleased the dominant. What pleased him even more was watching her porcelain skin turn rosy, each welt raising slightly with soft hairs standing up.

The dominant hung the crop back and reached for the flogger. "Color?" he asked again, ensuring his submissive was pleasantly happy with his delicious torture.

Melissa was quiet for a while as she collected her thoughts. "Green, Sir," she finally said, licking her lips. She swallowed hard and licked her lips again. He couldn't see her eyes behind the black satin blindfold, but her parted lips, rosy cheeks, and the sweat peppering her forehead told him exactly where she was.

The dominant loved it when a submissive reacted this way; when they were well on their way into the depths of their inner, yet soft, darkness. To a place where they felt safe, secure, and utterly comfortable. A place where they forgot about the world, a place where they thought about nothing but the pleasures he inflicted on her body. This place was their subspace; and he held the key to unlocking the ecstasy of her deep submission.

Melissa moaned with each whip of the dominant's soft leather flogger. It didn't hurt, but with a flick of his wrist, the ends of the leather tails whipped flesh, creating a sharp, short bite. He continued his pleasurable assault on her back, creating a rhythmic dance of leather against her skin, sending her further into the dark depths of her inner soul.

He returned the flogger on the wall, her back and buttocks a deep red, and closed the gap between them, pausing to let the anticipation build. In a single fluid move a ponytail twisted around one hand, snapping her head to one side. He thrusted his tongue down her throat, owning her; and his little submissive absorbed him, moaning softly in his kiss, intensifying when his free hand reached down between her legs held wide by spreader bars.

A finger continued teasing her, playing with that little button between her legs, but before sending her over the edge, he tightened the belt around her neck, ensuring the chain and locket were out of the way. Melissa's mouth opened as she fought to take in air. He licked her top lip, and pressed the Hitachi Magic Wand against her swollen clit until sparks flew and she cried out when her orgasm smashed into her over and over again.

The belt around her neck tightened even more, cutting off her air completely. The satin blindfold was lifted so she could see him. Melissa stared at him with pleading eyes, unable to loosen the restraints herself. She convulsed and shook but nothing helped, and the more the belt tightened, the more she thrashed around until finally her oxygen-starved body stilled, her eyes unseeing.

Chapter Two

A HIKER'S SURPRISE

Donovan caught up to his barking dog and rubbed his head. "Who's a good boy?" Donovan said, rubbing his dog behind his ears. "Yes, you're a good boy. Now what are you barking at?"

Donovan glanced up at the crown shyness of the trees and smiled, even in nature trees avoided each other much like himself avoiding his problems, and other people. Instead, he preferred hiking with Bob by his side.

The air smelled of pines, wet leaves, and rain, even though there wasn't a cloud in the sky. He inhaled deeply, exhaled, and shivered. His frown deepened as he raised his head and sniffed again. There was the smell again, which he couldn't place.

"Is that what you're smelling, Bob?" Donovan said, connecting the leash to his dog's collar. As much as he loved watching Bob run around on his own, that smell left him worried and wanted to ensure Bob's safety as much as his own. He sniffed again and cringed. "That's a nasty stench, boy."

Bob barked again and pulled Donovan off the Sawtooth Forest hiking trail near Bald Mountain. Donovan yanked on the leash to slow Bob down, but the dog was adamant that they reached the offending area immediately.

Donovan followed Bob, who sniffed under logs, around bushes, and near trees, until finally they reached an area where the stench was greatest. The ground at their feet had dried leaves strewn everywhere, but what laid on top made Donovan gag and turn around.

Bob continued sniffing and pawing at the animal carcass. From the looks of it, another predator had ripped the animal apart and left it there for later; or that's what Donovan thought and a reason he wanted to leave.

"Come now," Donovan said, yanking on the leash. "Leave it alone."

Bob continued pawing at the carcass on top of the mound of leaves, moving dirt around, and revealing something that made Donovan's blood drain from every part of his body. He couldn't tear his eyes away from the fingers sticking out of the ground or the worn, dark maroon polish on her nails.

Donovan swallowed the lump in his throat and pulled the leash hard enough to make Bob yelp and sit near his owner. Crouching, Donovan picked up a stick and poked at the hand and quickly realized it was human and not a mannequin he had hoped it was. He jumped backward, tripping over a rock, and fell hard on his bum. Donovan bolted upright and glanced around, ensuring he was the only one here, and pulled out his cell phone.

Chapter Three

THE BODY DUMP

Detective Steve Campbell

I placed my dishes in the sink and turned in time to catch Alice by her waist before she exited the kitchen and pulled her in for an embrace.

"It's a pity you need to leave," she said with her arms around my neck, glancing up at me. She gave me a look that tore at my heartstrings, and I'd do anything to stay at home with her for a day and garden or go for a walk or even just sitting around talking. Her light-brown eyes held sadness, and I wanted to kiss the hurt away.

I leaned forward and kissed her on the tip of her nose. "I'll be home for dinner," I said, smiling. With everything she had gone through, I enjoyed keeping things light at home and not so serious. "What are your plans for today?" I asked in a cheerful tone.

"Not sure, but I might go to the market today," she said, resting her head against my chest and squeezed me.

We had moved to Ketchum eight months ago, and with

each passing week, she started leaving the house more frequently. Last year, Alice had suffered two miscarriages, and the doctor advised us not to try again for a few months. Ever since then, she hadn't been well, and had been deteriorating by falling into a deep depression.

Then, the last case I had worked on, the man responsible for kidnapping all those women, had sent Alice a sunflower, a way to threaten me into leaving him alone. To protect Alice, I asked a doctor to admit Alice into high care at the local hospital to keep her safe but also to treat her. It was short of a miracle what he had done for her because a few days later she came home a little healthier and happier.

Although she wasn't herself one hundred percent, she was healing one day at a time, and when she had good days like today and ventured out, it warmed my heart. That meant that one day soon I'd have my Alice back. The woman I fell in love with in school, and love still. What we had was something different, in my mind. It was a love that connected us on a soul level, and not just skin deep.

"Have a good day at the market," I said, kissing her forehead.

"Do you know what kind of scene it is?" she asked, looking up at me with concern etched on her face.

"They found something near Bald Mountain in Sawtooth Forest they want me to look at."

"I hope it's not bad," she said solemnly, glancing away.

Not wanting to make her day worse, I smiled, cupped her face, and kissed her gently. "I'll see when I get there." She knew I solved homicide cases for a living; therefore I said nothing else about any new case I worked on. From experience, anything found in or near a forest usually meant it was a murder scene. Alice had been through enough. The last thing she needed now was to hear about a woman brutally tortured and murdered.

I parked my car behind Officer Graham's vehicle; it was the only one with a pink bunny on the back window; it was something his 4-year-old toddler had demanded he left in his personal car for protection.

I smiled at the thought of having a toddler running around giving me teddies to keep me safe, then sadness washed over me because we may never have a child of our own. We could always adopt, but I would first see how Alice recovered before bringing up the subject. Any topic that revolved around children made her teary and, although I wasn't in a rush to have a child, we were both in our forties, which made things difficult for us.

I walked past his vehicle to get to the hiking trail and remembered why I was here. Although I'd been to many crime scenes, this time it felt different; Alice still needed me at home, but I needed to work. This would be my third case in Ketchum, and a hiker and his dog found the body off the hiking trail, and the way Officer Graham had explained the crime scene it left me on edge.

"Detective," James McIntosh said, our lab technician who always got to scenes before me. "How's Alice doing?"

"Better every day," I said, shaking his gloved hand. "How was your vacation?"

"Those four days in Hawaii were so wonderful that I've already booked our next trip there," he said, grinning. "If hubby had found a job while we were there, he would've taken it on the spot and we'd move without thinking twice."

He took the disposable gloves off and threw them in a trash bag he was carrying.

"It would be our loss," I said, walking on the hiking path beside him. "Aren't you happy here?"

"It's not me, Detective," James said, staring at his boots as we walked. "Hubby needs to get out of the situation he's in. His boss is toxic, the environment is toxic. Everything about that place is awful."

"I hope he finds something closer, though. Not sure what we would do without you," I said sincerely. James was a wonderful crime scene technician, and it would be a significant loss to the team if he chose to leave.

James smiled. "Thanks," he glanced in my direction, "I appreciate that."

"What do we have?" I said, changing the subject and jerking my chin in the direction we were heading.

He shook his head and handed me a fresh pair of disposable gloves. "He covered her in a shallow grave with the carcass of a fox on top of her body."

"I wonder if he did that to hide her scent?"

"Probably," James said, walking off the path. "She has ligature marks all over her body."

I frowned. "Do you think they used rope?"

"I'm not sure. Probably. But I think the new coroner is best to answer your questions."

I'd forgotten about the new coroner starting today. "Dr. R. Brink," I said, more to myself than to James.

"Yep, we said our goodbyes to Doc Lesley early this morning when he came in to fetch his belongings and introduced us to the new Doc. She seems nice."

I stared at James as we walked, thinking the R was for Richard, but apparently the R in Dr. R. Brink was for someone female. I smiled to myself. We had more than enough men in the department. Having a female coroner would be a breath of fresh air.

"Over here," James said, pointing at his equipment on the ground, the bright lights on the scene, and where her body was.

"Morning," Officer Graham said, tipping his head, placing a marker on the ground, then placing the wrapper inside an evidence bag for processing.

"Morning," I said. "Is it just us today?"

"Yeah, Officer Crick is searching the area, and the other lab technicians are busy with another scene, so I'm helping James collect evidence."

I stood a distance away from the crime scene and glanced around. The killer had placed the victim near a large tree far from the hiking trail but still close to the parking area, and covered her with dirt and leaves. The roots of the tree seemed to shield her body from the elements, almost hugging her in nature's coffin. It was a strange scene to witness. Something I'd never seen before.

James continued collecting evidence while Officer Graham placed markers around the scene. Officer Graham took pictures and collected evidence that might reveal something, but I doubted it. Some of the wrappers collected could've been left there by other hikers.

I stepped closer to the victim to see what we were dealing with and I did everything I could not to turn away. Sand and leaves dirtied her knotty blond hair. Her blue-colored eyes were no longer vibrant but dull and unseeing. There were bruises along both sides of her jaw, on the left-hand side of her cheek, and a cut above her left eyebrow. Then, glancing lower, there was bruising around her neck, wrists, and ankles. The killer had sliced her right breast, splitting it in two. It seemed barbaric and done in anger.

She was slightly on the large side yet seemed healthy, apart from being murdered.

"Do you think the killer had strangled her to death?" I asked James, who was collecting evidence off her body.

"I honestly don't know," he said, shaking his head. "The killer had sexually assaulted her and there are wounds on her back."

I sucked in a deep breath of forest air and walked around the markers Officer Graham had placed on the ground. Glancing up, I noticed the trees above us kept their distance from the next tree. The air was cool, with a fine mist rolling in from the north. The hiking path was a few meters away which, when traversing it, one could enjoy breathtaking views of Ketchum, but there was nothing enjoyable about this view.

"Do we have a name for her?" I asked, standing near James.

"Melissa King, twenty-nine years old," James said, raising the evidence bag holding her identity, then he placed it in the box with the rest of the items he had collected. "At least the killer was decent enough to leave her handbag with all her things inside. It makes our job slightly easier." I detected a hint of sarcasm and I didn't blame him. The sooner we identified victims the sooner we could notify relatives.

The longer I stared at the victim, the angrier I became. "Christ, who did she provoke to suffer such a savage killing?" I asked, swallowing my breakfast that threatened to repeat on me.

James stood and dusted leaves and soil off his gloves. "My sister's kid is her age," he said sadly. "They even have similar hair color." He pointed at our victim's hair, then quickly glanced away.

In our line of work we shouldn't find resemblance in a victim to a family member. Usually it made our work that much harder. But it was difficult to not be human and to see the victim as a person we might have known. I needed to focus on something else and started making notes in my book.

"I think I got them all," Officer graham said, placing evidence bags in the box for James.

"Thanks," James said, crouching again. "I should be done soon and then I'll remove her body when the coroner arrives."

"Detective!" Officer Crick yelled.

I spun around as he jogged toward us. "What did you find?" I asked, closing the gap.

"I found a shrine of sorts," he pointed to my right, "and I think I found a pool of blood." He stopped walking to catch his breath and thumbed behind him.

"Well, come on. Show me," I said, jogging past him.

Officer Crick groaned, turned around, and caught up to me.

"Officer Graham!" I yelled, calling him over. "We'll need help to collect evidence for James."

"Take this," James called out to Officer Graham, who waited for the items. "And take pictures before you collect."

"Will do," Officer Graham said, running after us.

Chapter Four

THE SHRINE

Detective Steve Campbell

The area where we assumed they had killed the victim was only a few meters away from where we found her. Here they had made a shrine, and I crouched to get a better look. There were bones wrapped in a string around sticks and rocks, and a shell filled with a liquid I assumed was dried blood. It seemed simplistic at first glance, but I knew little about shrines or if it related to our victim.

There were tracks in various directions going to and from the shrine area that seemed to stop near our victim's body, while other tracks disappeared into the forest. It would take us time following each track thoroughly, but it had to be done; one of them could lead us to another crime scene.

I made notes in my book and walked around the area, noting that most of the trees here—like the one by our victim—had roots growing above ground, making them life-like. Their wood-like-fingers reaching out to grab an ankle or foot.

There were brown leaves still on the ground while on the trees, bright green leaves blossomed. The air smelled like fresh rain, wet trees, and leaves, with the sound of a stream nearby. I headed for the stream, approaching dark rocks gathered on one side.

"Officer Graham," I called. "I need you to collect some evidence." I closed the gap and leaned forward as Officer Graham neared.

"What is it?" he asked, standing on the other side of the rocks.

I called him over. "This looks like blood," I pointed at the dark red marks on the rock, "and that could be someone's clothing." I pointed at a torn piece of material. "Our victim is naked."

I stood back, giving Officer Graham space to take pictures of the area and to collect the evidence.

"They could've torn her clothing from her body and taken it with them," Officer Graham said, holding up the bag with the torn black cloth.

I smiled. "You could be right. I'll widen the search. Maybe there's more out here." I crossed the stream and headed toward a disturbed area. "It looks as though someone was attacked here, there, and then dumped her over there, or it's completely unrelated," I said, pointing at the various spots. "I'm going to walk this way around. Maybe I'll see something else."

"I'll drop these with James quickly and return."

I followed tracks that went from the shrine area directly to the stream and rocks, which I assumed resulted from our killer tracking our victim down. Some trees had broken branches where either our victim or killer had grabbed for support. But looking at the broken branches, I noted a new leaf growing, which left me feeling confused. I was unsure whether it related to our victim at all. Regardless, the results would reveal much.

I saw no other D.N.A. traces other than what looked like the blood on the rocks, and when the tracks seemed to disappear in a sea of footprints, I knew I'd reached the shrine area. Here they had also made a huge bonfire, even though the rules had forbidden it.

Following the next track, which went from the shrine area down one side of the mountain, and then stopped. There was nothing of interest here, so I backtracked.

The other track went from the back end of the shrine, down the mountain, and curved into dense vegetation. One section seemed denser, darker with rocks on one side, like there might be a cave, and I wanted to check it out, but I had no flashlight with me. I cursed under my breath; I couldn't believe I had forgotten my flashlight.

I traversed back to the shrine area just as Officer Crick started taking pictures and leaving markers where evidence needed to be collected. When I had first met him, I wasn't too sure about the type of person he was and the more I worked with him; it felt like I knew him even less.

"How are things coming along?" I asked, closing the gap.

"I found beads over there," he pointed at a bush near the shrine, "and two cigarette butts over there," he said, averting his eyes and placed a marker near the butts.

I pocketed my notebook and pen. "I've only been to one crime scene involving shrines. What about you?"

"We've had a couple, you know," he said, waving his hand in the air. "I think the land here attracts those more spiritual than others, but this is my first case that has a shrine."

"How come?" I asked, my interest piqued, especially if he said it happened more often here.

"Pure coincidence, really. Every time a case like this came up, I was busy taking care of my mother," he said sadly.

"Did she recover or did her condition worsen?"

"She passed away last year," he said sadly. "She'd been sick since I was in high school."

"I'm sorry," I offered. If I had to guess, Officer Crick was in his late twenties. He still had that smooth jawline and no crow's feet near his eyes, but he had some scars. "That must have been tough on you, considering it lasted so long. What about your father?"

He shook his head. I thought he was about to say more when he moved farther away from me.

"Sorry, I didn't mean to pry," I said, moving in the opposite direction.

"It's not that, Detective," Officer Crick said, finally looking at me. "It's just I haven't spoken about it in a long time and you're new here. I don't know what your angle is or why you're asking me so many questions."

"I only want to get to know the people I work with. My mother would moan at me if I didn't engage with my colleagues and tell me to stop being rude," I said, smiling. "And don't sweat it. If you don't want to answer any of my questions, you don't have to." I pointed up ahead. "I'm going to go back this way and see if I find anything."

"If you really want to know, my dad was never in the picture," he added, "and Mom got sick the year I started my senior classes, and she died last year. We were poor and had nobody to help me clean, feed, and medicate her. And when she died in my arms, there was some comfort; that she was finally pain free, and that she was able to watch me become a police officer to rid this earth of people who didn't deserve a life better than those they hurt." Red blotches spread across his neck and face, and his black brows creased. His hair was so black that his brown eyes seemed lighter now that his face was red.

I wasn't sure if his reaction was because of his mother dying or his father deserting him. "Did someone hurt your mother?"

He pursed his lips, and his jaw ticked. "Before my father left, he forced himself on my mother, giving her a deadly gift. They found his body six months later, naked in an alley with a needle in his arm, while my mother had to suffer on top of her comorbidity conditions." He mumbled something I strained to hear. "I worked two jobs to keep the lights on and to ensure nobody took my mom's house away."

"It must have been incredibly difficult for someone so young to take on so much."

One never really understood the magnitude somebody had to go through to survive daily, nor did we fully comprehend the severity. Officer Crick usually gave me this strange vibe, but what he revealed about himself provided me with the bigger picture, and the vibe I got from him now was that of a man who overcame his struggles. He was terribly skinny, with scars on his knuckles, his temple, and across his chin I assumed were defensive wounds. He had overcome a lot in his young life.

Officer Crick caught me staring at his hands and pulled up his sleeves, revealing more scars. "You might as well know the truth, Detective. I've already disclosed this to my superior. I took part in illegal bare-knuckle boxing. Nobody got seriously hurt, and I was part of the task team to close it down."

"Aren't you scared?" I asked, stepping closer. "Those types of fights are usually mafia driven."

"Not this one. It was a father and son team offering these matches in their home."

"Do you know where they are now?"

"They're both in jail."

"And you aren't worried they'll come looking for you?"

"They don't know who it was, and they know little about me." He stepped closer. His brown-colored eyes piercing mine. "Only two people know about this, and now three. If anything happens, I'll know it was you."

"Is that a threat, Officer Crick?" I asked, standing taller, staring down at him. I hated pissing contests, but when someone threatened me like Officer Crick just did, I never backed down.

"No, Detective," he said, puffing out his chest. "I'm only informing you that my superior and me would never say a word. And now you're the third. That is all." He shrugged nonchalantly and placed a marker on the ground. "I'm a police officer. I don't threaten, I only react to danger," he said this part without looking at me.

Sighing, I shook my head. I had to be careful of this one. "I'm heading back," I said, and traversed a path we had made that went on the outskirts of the shrine area and then headed back to where we found the victim's body. As I approached, James was speaking with the new coroner, Dr. R. Brink.

"Detective Steve Campbell," James said. "This is Dr. Rachel Brink, our new coroner."

Dr. Brink closed the gap. She was in her mid-forties with jet-black hair, high cheek bones, and a beauty spot near her left green eye. She reminded me of Dita Von Teese; their similarities were striking.

She proffered a hand, which I shook gently, while she almost crushed my knuckles. "Call me Rachel. And you, Detective," she said, "I've heard a lot of good things and I look forward to working with you."

"That's good to know. I wish I could say the same about you, though." I smiled and rubbed my hand. "I know nothing about you, but I, too, look forward to working with you."

"I'm originally from Ketchum," she started, "studied and worked in New York, and now I'm back here. I love bugs, and I hope to get your victim prepped and completed by tomorrow." She glanced down at our victim and tsk'ed. "I may have some theories," she added. "But let me first perform a proper autopsy." She crouched near the body.

We stood around, watching Rachel as she worked. She checked the body temperature, and could easily raise the victim's arm, which meant rigor mortis hadn't set in yet.

"Time of death is roughly six this morning," Rachel said to nobody specifically, but I took out my notebook to write notes. "She was bound by her ankles, wrists, and neck." She pointed at the deep bruise around the victim's neck. "And most likely strangled." She opened the victim's eyelids farther, revealing petechial hemorrhaging.

"The killer did a number on her right breast," she said, shaking her head. "No idea what they had used, but it wasn't sharp. Look how it tore the skin and tissue. Barbaric." She shook her head.

Rachel stood and asked James to assist her in turning the body. When they did that myself, Officer Graham and Officer Crick stepped backward, and I held a hand in front of my face. I thought her breast was horrific. The victim's back showed signs of repeated torture; it looked like tiny welts on her back that had drawn blood, and they had removed pieces of her flesh in the shape of a leaf.

"The victim was still alive when they did that," she said, shaking her head and pointing at the missing flesh. "They tortured this poor woman relentlessly."

"Do you think it was cult related?" I asked, folding my arms across my chest.

"Anything is possible right now, Detective."

"We found a shrine back there, so maybe."

She glanced up at me and her smile reached her eyes. "That shrine could've been there before this happened or it's related. Like I've said, I'll need to perform an autopsy, but even then, it may not have any relation to our victim."

I felt my cheeks heat and all I could do was smile and nod. "Thanks."

She stood and retrieved a bag. "I'll give you more once I've done the sexual assault forensic exam. But from what I can tell, just looking at her, it was pretty bad." She crouched again. "Help me, James."

James nodded and together they carefully placed her body inside the bag and zipped it closed. They stood, reached for the handles on the side, and picked up the body.

Officer Graham carried the evidence bags that needed to go with them while Officer Crick and I stood back.

Chapter Five

THE CAVE

Detective Steve Campbell

"Can I use your flashlight?" I asked, pointing at the item on Officer Crick's belt.

Officer Crick narrowed his eyes, but did as I asked and handed me his flashlight. "What do you need it for?" he asked, frowning.

"There's a spot I found when I was following the various paths," I said, pointing behind him, "and I'm curious to explore more, but I'll need light. It may be nothing. Would you like to join me? I might need your help."

Officer Crick nodded. "Sure, why not. I doubt I need to stay here." He motioned for me to walk ahead.

We traversed the path I'd taken earlier and stopped when we reached the thick vegetation and the area where it looked like there might be a cave.

"Wow," Officer Crick said. "I've hiked here many times before, yet never seen this," he pointed. "There really is a cave over there." He walked ahead of me, taking his keys out of his pocket and flicking on a tiny flashlight. "I always come prepared," he said over his shoulder, jingling his car keys.

I switched on the flashlight he had given me and shone it on the leaves covering the ground. The vegetation was so dense we stepped on roots, thick layers of leaves, and broken branches to get to the opening of the cave.

Officer Crick entered the cave first. His tiny light struck small parts of the cave. I entered behind him and pointed the flashlight, which cast a larger shine, illuminating the dark cave.

The smell of damp soil wafted in the air, along with a sour stench which could result from vomit or a dead animal. We traversed deeper inside the bowels of the cave, finding nothing untoward, until we reached the back of the cave.

"I don't believe it," I said as we stopped when we reached another shrine with similar bones tied with string on sticks. There was another white shell with dried liquid inside, two earrings that didn't match each other, and a worn leather collar. There was damp paper underneath it all, and I wanted to get a better look.

"This must be related," Officer Crick said, leaning over the shrine.

"Do you have the camera with you?"

"Yep," he said, pulling it out of his pocket.

"Can you take a few snaps before I push items around? I want to see what's beneath it all."

Officer Crick did as I asked and took pictures of the shrine; some at a distance, some close ups, then of the various items resting on the rock.

With my pen, I pushed the shell to one side and shone the flashlight on the newspaper below. The newspaper featured a story from last year about a woman found tortured and murdered in a forest. This discovery sent a chilling sensation through my veins. It felt like I was reading about our victim, only it happened in a different forest.

"Intriguing," was all I could say. I had no words to describe the similarities; it was unbelievable. I pushed the shell farther out of the way so I could read the next newspaper clipping.

"Here's another one," Officer Crick said. "Which forest does that one say they found the victim?"

Narrowing my eyes as I scanned the article. "They're both Gunnison National Forest in Colorado."

"So is this one." He pushed sticks and bones to the other side and read the next newspaper. "This is also Gunnison. Do we know where our victim is from?"

"Not yet," I said. "I'd like to know more about these women though, and what connects them to our victim other than our killer."

"Let me go back and get evidence bags."

"Thanks," I said as Officer Crick exited the cave, leaving me alone. I shone the light on the shrine, then followed the rocky wall to the left, illuminating the ground and the various rock formations, until I had searched the entire cave area. Apart from the shrine, there was nothing but sticks, leaves, sand, and stones. There were no wrappers, cigarette butts, or anything noteworthy for testing.

Sweat peppered my forehead, and my clothing clung to my body. I needed fresh air and headed for the mouth of the cave. When I reached the exit, I sucked in a deep breath of forest air, filling my lungs, and exhaled. Under different circumstances, I would've enjoyed the scenic view of the green trees, atmosphere, and lush vegetation. Instead, my mind wandered to the victim and what she had gone through. There was a cult in the area sacrificing women, and if the newspapers on this shrine were anything to go by, the killer or killers seemed to move from one forest to the next.

Footsteps crunching leaves sounded, and I reached for my gun.

"It's just me," Officer Graham said, approaching. "Officer Crick said you found another shrine." He smiled when he saw me.

"Yep, I was just thinking we may have a cult operating in these woods and I don't know the first thing about them."

"Let's first see what we have here," Officer Graham said, entering the cave and switching on his flashlight. "Officer Crick is just finishing a few things at the primary crime scene and asked that I bag some evidence. Now what do we have here?" he said, placing the shell, bones, sticks and string inside a bag. Then he pulled out a fresh bag, collected the newspaper clippings, and carefully placed them inside their individual bags for processing.

"Did you get everything?" I asked, shining the flashlight around the shrine.

"Yep," he said. "Now, can we get out of here? This place gives me the creeps." He shuddered for effect and headed for the exit.

"I couldn't agree more." I stopped and pointed the light at the wall above the shrine. "Wait!" I yelled.

"What is it?"

"What do you see there on the rocks?"

Officer Graham returned to stand beside me. "Is that a word, or are my eyes playing tricks on me?"

I stepped backward until the light revealed more. "It looks like a word. Can you take a picture, or should I use my cell phone?"

"It's okay, I have the camera." He had a better digital

camera than Officer Crick did, and every time he took a picture, he looked at the small screen on the back. "It's so dark and I don't know if it's dirt, but if I had to guess, it spells 'MINE'." He shrugged and showed me the screen.

The rocks were dirty with what looked like grime smeared all over it, but I could clearly see the distinct pattern of each letter disturbing the grime. I nodded. "It looks like it spells 'MINE'."

"Do you think it's written in blood?"

"I would be surprised if it wasn't."

Officer Graham continued collecting samples from each letter, as well as the grime used.

"Do you enjoy forensics?" I asked when he was done.

"I enjoy both parts of it, you know, collecting the evidence, then going after the bad guy."

I chuckled. "Yeah, I just like going after the bad guy."

Chapter Six

THE SEARCH

Detective Steve Campbell

Since I started working at Ketchum Police station, I'd interacted with Officer Graham most of the time and he was a valuable resource who was slowly becoming a friend. Although life dealt him a raw deal when they caught his father dealing drugs and then later killed himself, Officer Graham's work ethics were of the best standards, and he was one of the best people I'd ever worked with.

I sat across from him eating my chicken mayo salad even though I craved a juicy red steak. Apparently, I needed to lose a few pounds. To assist me, Alice had made me salads for lunch; her way of ensuring I didn't buy takeout.

"The purse we found near the victim had her I.D. and based on the system she lived in Boise—"

"What is she doing all the way here?" I asked, confused.

"It's less than a three-hour drive," Officer Graham said in a tone I'd associate with arrogance. "The killer probably dropped her body here to throw us off."

"I know that," I said, feeling annoyed. "But why here?" I rubbed my face with my free hand. "They have the Boise National Forest."

Officer Graham shrugged. "Maybe that's what the killer does."

"What? Confuse cops."

"Yeah," he said, picking up copies of the newspaper clippings we had retrieved from the cave. "I still need to check these out." We had sent the original clippings for processing and would only get the results by the end of the week, hopefully.

Reaching for one article written by the local newspaper in Gunnison, I read through it carefully. "I hate to point out the obvious, but this victim has similarities to our case." I raised the clipping for Officer Graham to see.

"And this one," Officer Graham said. "Let me investigate properly. Perhaps you should reach out to Boise Police Department and let them know we found one of their residents in our forest."

"Yeah," I said. "Let me get that out of the way."

As I left Ketchum, I dialed Alice's number on my hand-free kit.

"Hey love, how is it going?" she asked, sounding perky.

"It's okay," I said. I always said a case was going okay, even if it wasn't. I rarely shared details of any case with her. She was a very sensitive person and hearing about any of my cases usually left her emotionally drained and sad for a few days.

"I'm on my way to Boise—"

"Boise?" she asked, her voice raised. "Why Boise?"

"Just following up on some leads."

"Can the police there not help you?"

"They are, but it's something I need to check out myself."

"Hmm, okay," she said, sounding deflated.

"I'm just calling to let you know I might be home a little late tonight, but I'll try to be home by six."

"I'll keep your dinner in the oven for you," she said, her tone a little more cheerful.

"What have you been up to?"

"I went to the market for fresh vegetables and I'm busy making roast beef with potatoes."

I could almost smell the food through the cell phone. "That sounds delicious, and I can't wait to get home."

"Be safe."

"I will," I said, smiling even though I knew she couldn't see me. "Love you."

"Love you, too."

It was 1 p.m. by the time I arrived at Boise Police Department and Detective Phillip Marshall welcomed me. He was a big fellow with a shaved head and a bushy red beard. His uniform seemed a little too small for the muscles straining against the shirt, but he had a kind smile and warm blue eyes. He reminded me of a teddy bear with a gun.

"Detective Campbell," Detective Marshall said, shaking my hand and slapping me on my shoulder. "Come with me to my office so I can grab my keys, then we can go in my car."

"Sure," I said, following him down a corridor and into a

large office where others were busy. I would've preferred driving in my vehicle and following him there. That way I could leave and head back home, but I was polite and wanted to make new police friends; one never knew when he could come in handy, and he probably wanted to get to know me, too.

"I must say," he started, "I'm surprised to hear about this murder. We have quite a low murder rate in the area."

"Tell me about it," I said. "Before I moved to Ketchum, there had been no murders for years. Now this is my second homicide case in the first year," I said, shaking my head. "And I'd like to resolve this one before there's another." I hoped there wouldn't be another murder. By moving to Ketchum, I had hoped to solve cases involving theft or break-ins that were stress free, but it seemed life had other plans for me.

"Right," Detective Marshall said to himself as he searched for his car keys on his messy desk. "Here we go," he said, glancing at me, then headed for the exit to his left. "I looked up the victim, Melissa King," he pushed open the door and descended the stairs, "blond hair, blue eyes, and lives alone. She's recently divorced, has no kids, and her ex agreed to meet us at his office in an hour." He glanced at his watch, then pushed the basement door open.

We traversed down the stairs and reached the basement level. I climbed into his police vehicle and before I could close my door, we were out of the parking area. Detective Marshall focused on the road and didn't say a word. I glanced out of the window at the views Boise had to offer. It was only when we stopped outside an apartment block did Detective Marshall speak.

"Deven, her ex, gave us permission to enter the apartment they used to share. He moved out six months ago and kept his key, which he has left under the welcome mat. Apparently, he watches too many television programs and didn't want us breaking any doors down." He chuckled. "He said he would try to excuse himself from work to meet us here, but if not, we can speak with him at his office."

Detective Marshall lifted the straw mat, retrieved the spare key, and opened the front door. Everything was neat and tidy. It was a two-bedroom apartment with a small balcony. There was a two-seater couch in front of a television, a bookshelf, and a four-seater dining room table and then an open-plan kitchen.

Nothing seemed out of the ordinary; there was nothing for me to believe that a struggle took place here. Either Melissa knew her attacker or her torture took place elsewhere.

I checked the kitchen while Detective Marshall entered her bedroom. I closed the cupboard when a whistle sounded. Wanting to know what he found, I entered the neat bedroom but stopped in the doorjamb.

"What the hell is that?" I asked, confused. I cocked my head to the side, trying to make sense of what he held in his hands.

"It's a type of outfit."

"It looks like a feral cat attacked a black bag," I said, narrowing my eyes. I wasn't a prude, and I had my fair share of exploration, but I'd never dived into this scene before, nor had there ever been a case involving such things.

"B.D.S.M has its place in all towns and Boise is no different," Detective Marshall said, shaking the garment, "and I guess your victim had a kinky side to her." He hung the leather strapped outfit back in her closet. "Did you find anything?"

"No, but I was about to check the second bedroom

when you whistled." I left Detective Marshall in Melissa's bedroom and entered the second bedroom she used as an office.

She had a MacBook Air open on a white table and an open appointment book. In the diary marked for yesterday, she was scheduled to meet someone named *'Monsieur'* at seven last night. I flipped through the pages and there were hair appointments, doctor appointments, a few lunch dates with clients and, based on that, I suspected she had her own company and was an online marketer for a few companies.

I opened the closet, finding posters for products and spare paper. On one wall was a board listing the various companies I recognized from her appointment book.

The drawers in her table had nothing of interest, and her MacBook was password protected. Hopefully, her ex knew how to get into it.

"Find anything interesting?" Detective Marshall asked, sticking his head inside the room. He whistled. "What's all this?"

"She's a marketing manager or brand manager," I waved my hand near the wall, "and comes up with slogans for products. But that's not the interesting part," I picked up the diary and showed him yesterday's entry. "She was going to meet a *'Monsieur'*."

Detective Marshall frowned. "It's French for Sir, Mister, or Gentleman," he said. "And if that outfit in her room means what I think it does, then she was going to meet someone from the kink scene." He stomped farther inside the room, taking the diary out of my hands. "Now all we have to do is figure out who *'Monsieur'* really is."

Chapter Seven

DEVEN KING

Detective Steve Campbell

Deven King was not the type of man I was expecting to see, considering the reason Melissa divorced him; infidelity. He sauntered up to us with his hand held out in front of him like the confident man he was. His hands were cold and clammy, and he used too much force; perhaps overcompensating for something.

After the introductions and we sat around his conference table inside his office, he steepled his fingers. He wore a perfectly pressed suit and a maroon tie. He had combed over the few strands of hair he still had on top of his head to one side and his brown-colored bug eyes penetrated mine. It felt like a pissing contest.

Deven King was your typical defense lawyer; he had enough charisma to charm any young paralegal out of her stockings, but there was something I couldn't quite place.

"Did you find anything in Melissa's apartment that

could explain what happened to her?" he asked, glancing at his watch.

"Mr. King," I started, "you seem to be in a hurry. Did we catch you at a bad time to talk about your ex, whom we found brutally tortured and murdered? They dumped her body in Sawtooth Forest like garbage."

Deven King had entered his office a confident lawyer, but after my outburst, his facade started crumbling. "If you think I did anything to hurt poor Melissa, you're wrong," he yelled, breaking a glass. Then he stood up, knocking his chair over. His face was red and blotchy and when both Detective Marshall and I reached out for him, he held his hands up in surrender.

After ten minutes, Deven King finally calmed down, picked up his chair and fell into it as if he had no more energy left to maintain his confident facade.

"You're right, Detective," he started, shaking his head slightly, then wiped beads of sweat off his brow. "I messed up." Tears welled in his eyes. "I was the worst husband to Melissa, and I paid the price, but you must understand whatever happened to her wasn't me. I would never physically harm her, never mind kill her."

He stared out of the window, and after a couple of minutes, he glanced at me. "Why would anyone hurt her? She's the sweetest most loving person I've ever known."

"That's what we need to determine," Detective Marshall said, taking a business card out of his pocket and pushing it across the table. "Do you know who she met last night?"

Deven reached across the table and picked up the card. He flipped it over to see the number, then pocketed it.

"I haven't known what she's been up to for almost six or

seven months," he said solemnly. "I know I hurt her badly, so to make amends, I gave her the apartment, I pay her credit card with a monthly allowance, and I agreed to do all this until she remarried. And if she never remarried, that's okay, because we have a history and I never deserved her in the first place. She really was one of a kind and I messed things up."

"This is very difficult to ask," Detective Marshall said, glancing in my direction. I nodded, then he continued with his question. "Do you know if Melissa was involved in the kink scene here in Boise?"

Deven's brows arched. "Kink?" he asked, glancing from Detective Marshall to me. "What? No, we barely had sex during our marriage. Why do you think I cheated on her? She never wanted to do it much after we got married. Sometimes it felt as though she only had sex with me in the beginning of our relationship was because she wanted to get married. Then, after we said our vows, things just dried up." He was quiet for a while, then added. "So no, she had no interest in sex."

"Mr. King," I said. "We found outfits that suggested the opposite, and we found sex toys in a drawer." Before we left the apartment, I searched the bedroom while Detective Marshall searched the office to make sure we missed nothing. Which was a good thing because Detective Marshall neglected to search her chest of drawers and it was there where I found two drawers filled with sex toys and another filled with lingerie.

Deven stared deadpan at me with his lips slightly parted. When he realized he'd been staring, he closed his mouth and blinked. "I can't believe this," he said, shaking his head. "I simply can't. It's like I didn't even know her. I mean…"

he continued, shaking his head. "...how can she have changed so dramatically and so quickly? Kink? I can't believe it."

"Did she ever talk about someone named Monsieur?" I asked.

Deven shook his head. "No, never." After a moment's silence, he added, "Someone had to have made her do it, maybe this Monsieur fellow. That has to be the reason. Maybe he blackmailed her or something." He shrugged. "That has to be the reason." He seemed desperate to make the reason why she would rather have kinky sex with someone she barely knew than with him, was due to external forces beyond her control. I suspected it was a hard pill for him to swallow, knowing she had an interest in exploring that side of herself, but without him.

"We'll find out," Detective Marshall said, standing up. "If you think of anything else, please call."

"Yeah," Deven said, staring off into nothing.

I stood, pushed my chair in, and walked near the desk. On a shelf behind his chair stood a handful of photos and there was one with Melissa and Deven standing in front of a waterfall, but no photo that included a new girlfriend.

"When I heard Melissa had died, I put that photo back," Deven said behind me.

"Do you have a new girlfriend?" I asked, picking up the photo.

"No, in between at the moment."

I placed the photo back on the shelf and turned around, noting Deven had been crying. When I tried to walk around him, he blocked my path.

"Find who did this to her," he said, then choked on a sob.

I didn't know what to do, so I patted his shoulder. "We'll do everything we can to figure this out."

It was almost 3 p.m. and although I wanted to rush back home, I agreed to accompany Detective Marshall to a well-known sex shop that also rented out a kink dungeon.

"This is one shop I know many people frequent," Detective Marshall said. "And if they don't know our victim, I'm sure they'll be able to tell us where to go."

After Detective Marshall, I entered The Play Spot & Anonymous Dungeon and was pleasantly surprised at the layout of the sex shop. I was expecting black walls, sticky shelves, and a counter manned by a miserable, large, sweaty man named Brutus. Instead, they had painted the walls an eggshell color. One side had glass shelves with female toys, the other wall held metal shelves for male toys. In the center was a velvety-soft red chair, and at the back of the shop was the cash register where one could buy various accessories and pills.

To the left of the cash register was a door painted a deep-red with the name "Anonymous Dungeon" above the doorframe.

"Detective Marshall," said a woman on my right who had appeared from an aisle I hadn't noticed. My eyes were bouncing across the various toy-filled shelves as I tried hard not to attract any attention to my heated cheeks. "And you've brought someone with you," she said. Her voice was delicate enough to wrap her words around my face. "What will it be today."

I glanced wide-eyed at Detective Marshall, who smiled

sheepishly. Obviously, he was a regular and seemed open to admitting he was a kinky detective. A picture of him holding fluffy pink handcuffs filled my vision, and I tried not to grin.

"Violet," Detective Marshall said, kissing both her cheeks in greeting. "Not for pleasure today, I'm afraid." He pouted.

"Ah, that's no good. You haven't been here for a while," Violet said, placing a broken crop on the counter. "I've missed you." She wore a body-hugging black pencil skirt, and a maroon blouse that showed off her cleavage. Her black, curly hair was in a messy bun with loose strands of hair framing her delicate features. Although her body was on the bigger side, she dressed with confidence, which made her ooze sexiness, and her dark makeup made her green eyes pop.

"Work has been busy," he said, picking up a large silicone dildo, shaking it, and then put it back down. I chuckled to myself.

"What can I help you with today?" Violet said, staring from my shoes up my legs, chest until her eyes found my face, all the while smiling mischievously. Her staring at me like that wasn't creepy, and for a split second, I felt desired.

"I know you pride yourself on running a private business," Detective Marshall said, touching a feather, "but we need to know if you've seen this woman or know who we can speak with regarding her." He left the feather alone and held up a photo he'd taken from Melissa's apartment.

Violet visibly sighed, but took the photo out of his hands to look at it. "I don't like this," she said, handing it back to him and went behind the counter. "But I'll help you. What happened to her?"

"Detective Campbell over here found her brutally tortured and killed in Sawtooth Forest," he said.

Violet paled. "That's terrible." She swallowed hard. "Melissa is a new submissive," she added, reaching for a large black diary. She set the diary on the counter and opened it to yesterday's booking.

"You don't trust a computer for your bookings?" I said.

She peered at me and nodded. "These days, anyone can hack a system. Should the information in this book get leaked, it could ruin my business and those who come here; and some are very high-profile people. It will destroy reputations." She raised an eyebrow for effect. "This way, my book is in the safe, either here or at home." She searched the name with her long index fingernail, tapping the spot. "Here we go. She's a lovely girly. I mean, was a lovely girly. Very pleasant and kind." She shook her head.

"May I?" Detective Marshall said, holding his notebook and pen, and leaned over to see the name.

"Is your dungeon busy?" I asked, curious about something.

"Ever since I opened, I never have an open slot."

"How do you remember who was here and under which name?"

"Each person needs to be vetted by someone I know personally. Plus, I'm very good with faces and times, and that girl," she pointed at the photo Detective Marshall was still holding, "was here and under this name."

"Sensual Suzie," Detective Marshall mumbled.

"Who was she here with?" I asked.

"Monsieur." Violet tapped the name beside *Sensual Suzie's.*

"Do you know his real name or have his contact details?"

Violet shook her head. "No, I never keep contact details of anyone, and he's been here a couple of times. He always enters my shop with his mask already on." She glanced to my left.

I followed her line of sight, seeing the cameras. "Can we see?"

"Sure, but you won't see much."

Chapter Eight

MONSIEUR

Detective Steve Campbell

"Olivia!" Violet yelled.

A woman with brown hair, brown-colored eyes, and wearing a boring black tunic, entered from behind a curtain on the far side of the shop. "Yes, Violet," she said, glancing at me and then Detective Marshall.

"Watch the shop. We're just going to look at some security footage in my office."

"Sure," Olivia said, heading for the cash register.

We sat in Violet's office watching the video of Monsieur enter the shop and then he traversed along the dark corridor toward the dungeon. Once he was inside the dungeon, he removed his work shirt, revealing no markings or tattoos we could use to identify him. The mask he wore covered him from his nose and upward, leaving only his mouth and jaw open.

Violet had painted the dungeon a dark gray color with one wall a dark red. There were various soft-covered benches, beams, cages, and even a bed with metal posters and shackles attached to each corner. There was a red silk duvet and pillows on the bed, and a mini fridge beside it. The room seemed modern, yet medieval. The darkness of the room left me feeling slightly uncomfortable.

Melissa, otherwise known as Sensual Suzie, was already waiting patiently for him. She was naked, and kneeling on the floor with her hands in her lap, palms up, and staring at the ground. I would lie if I said it didn't remind me of a scene in that Fifty Shades movie. I couldn't remember which one of the three movies it was in, but that's what it looked like.

Monsieur grabbed his crotch, adjusting it, and stood in front of Melissa. He crouched and with his index finger raised her chin so she could look him in the eyes. There was no sound in the video, but it looked like he told her to look at him. When she did, he helped her to stand, cupped her face, and kissed her gently on her mouth. Then he reached for her hand and led her to a bench where he tied her wrists and ankles at the allocated leather cuffs, and reached for the flogger.

I flinched each time he hit her with the flogger, while Detective Marshall stared lustfully at the screen and Violet shifted in her seat. I didn't understand what was going on or why anyone would want to have this done to them, but it made me feel incredibly uncomfortable.

Violet fast-forwarded to the next scene where Melissa was now tied to a cross and tortured with a crop, then fingered, followed by being slapped in the face and on her breasts, and lastly bitten on each breast followed by a few bites on her stomach. He left no marks on her body, though.

After what felt like an hour, even though it was only fifteen minutes of his "torture", Monsieur freed her of her restraints, bent her over another bench and had intercourse with her; using each of her holes.

Monsieur and Melissa showered after their cuddle, and after he washed a part of her body, he planted a kiss until he had kissed her all over. This was the only time he had removed his mask but because the shower was in the far corner, we saw little of his face.

After three hours, they were done and left separately.

It felt like I'd watched a porn movie and now needed a shower or an exorcist to rid me of these dirty demons. I rubbed my face. "I must admit, I don't understand this. They aren't a couple, yet she allowed him to do so much to her. How? Why? I mean, look at that, it took a lot of trust to be tied up like that. He could've hurt her."

Violet shook her head. "They're just play partners, and you're right. It takes a lot to trust a Dominant to do all those things to a submissive. She must trust him enough not to hurt her when he's tied her. She's alone with him and unable to defend herself. Therefore, it's imperative I vet each person before they can play, because I don't want rapists, predators, or molesters in my dungeon." Her voice raised toward the end of her speech, letting me know she took this seriously. "And he has been vetted by me.," she said softer, shaking her head. "That's why it would be difficult for me to believe he killed her."

"We still need to question him," I said. "Help me understand," I continued. "Anonymous sex which includes using various toys and then they go their separate way?" I asked, feeling even more confused than before.

"They've played here a few times and I've only seen them play with each other. It is possible they play with other people elsewhere, but here, they've only played with each other. Therefore, the more often they play, the more comfortable they get with each other. It's actually quite common." She glanced at Detective Marshall, and I wanted to ask him questions but thought best to keep quiet… for now. Instead, my frown deepened.

"The world of kink is open to many sexual opportunities," Violet said. "There are businessmen who want to wear adult diapers, drink milk from a bottle, and have a female cuddle them while they slept. Female CEOs who spend their days managing others come here to submit to a Dominant. You can meet someone online, get to know them, then agree on what will happen at a play date or if you want more than just play. Each person decides what they want and then informs their Dominant or submissive. There are a lot of discussions and negotiations; it all depends on what each person is after."

"I don't suppose you have something on Kink for Dummies?" I asked, realizing how complicated this world really was and how I didn't fit into any category at all.

Violet smiled kindly. "It is overwhelming for outsiders to understand, but just remember this; it's about realizing fantasies and turning them into a reality. And, in some way, it's better than a normal relationship, because here you tell your partner from the beginning what you like and don't like. In a vanilla relationship, one only finds these things out years down the line."

"It makes sense," I said, contemplating what she had said. It took me and Alice years before we understood what the other wanted because we were too shy to say it outright. If I had to guess, communicating openly and honestly really was the best way, whether it was kink or vanilla.

I glanced at my watch and was eager to get home to Alice. After watching that video of Sensual Suzie and

Monsieur, I wanted to get home and give Alice the biggest and longest hug and kiss, and then enjoy a cold shower.

"Thank you for your time, Violet," Detective Marshall said, kissing the top of her hand.

Violet leaned into him and whispered something into his ear. They both laughed. She kissed his cheek, then turned to me.

"It was wonderful meeting you, Detective Campbell. Here's my card if you ever want to know more."

I took the card from her delicate fingers and pocketed it without looking at it. "Please call either of us when Monsieur enters your dungeon again. We'd like to speak with him."

"Absolutely," she said, smiling.

I doubted she would call me, but that didn't matter. Detective Marshall seemed to have a foot in the kink door, and I would accept any help I could get.

I slipped my key into the lock, turned, and opened the door. The smell of scones wafted in the air and a smile stretched my face.

"Hey honey," I said, dropping my bag and locking the front door. "That smells divine." I entered the kitchen as Alice took the tray of baked goods out of the oven and placed them on a cooling rack.

"You're home," she said, smiling. She set the oven mitts on the counter and wrapped her arms around my neck, and kissed me. "Was it that bad?"

"Yeah," I said, leaning forward, "something like that." I kissed her forehead, snaked my arm around her and grabbed a still very hot scone, but dropped it when it burned my fingertips, quickly sticking the burned digits into my mouth.

Alice spun around and smacked the top of my hand. "That's for after dinner," she chastised with a grin. "Did you burn?" she asked with concern, taking my hand in hers, searching for a blister.

"I'll be all right," I said, kissing her again. "How was your day?"

"Good, I made dinner," she said, heading for the fridge. She retrieved two bowls, and I groaned inwardly. Salad. It had to be salad. When she saw my face, she laughed. "Haha, it's roast beef with potatoes, silly, the salad goes on the side."

I smiled. "Good, because that sounds like just what I need today."

After I washed my hands, we enjoyed our dinner, sharing a bottle of Merlot. When we were done, we sat on the porch out back and enjoyed the cool evening and the quiet of the forest.

Every day that went by, I started loving this place, but the main thing was Alice was becoming more like the Alice from before her two miscarriages. We sat in the love swing, my arm around her shoulders, her head on my chest and her hand near my heart, and we sat in silence, absorbing each other's energies and the surrounding nature.

Chapter Nine

THE LAST PLACE

Detective Steve Campbell

During my visit to The Play Spot & Anonymous Dungeon yesterday, back at the station Officer Graham had pulled Melissa King's credit card records for clues leading up to her death. She had paid for all their play sessions at the Anonymous Dungeon, which we now knew was with Monsieur.

Then, after her last play session, she had stopped at another venue where she had paid for two tickets. Officer Graham searched what kind of venue it was, learning it was an erotic show. It wasn't so much hosted in a building in the city, but an event in the forest. A kink company from Boise, who had various B.D.S.M artists on display, hosted the events for the month.

Officer Graham and I arrived at the spot between Boise and Ketchum. It was near Doniphan on Poison Creek Road. The kink company; The Pleasure Zone, had banners up and had ring fenced a section of the beautiful land.

Waiting in the parking area stood a tall, cleanly shaven man wearing a jean jacket and black leather pants. He had his hands on his hips, pinching a toothpick between his thick lips. As we closed the gap, he turned in our direction and smiled.

"Detective," Craig Williams said, shaking my hand. "You're just in time." He greeted Officer Graham and headed for the entrance. "We're here for a couple more weeks and then we close before moving to another state." He pushed the reed door open.

Above the reed door sat a metal sign with glowing letters in neon pink that read *"The Pleasure Zone"* and beside it *"Kink In Nature"*. On either side of the sign and reed door were metal spiral staircases that seemed to be for decorative purposes. I couldn't see an office on top or on either side.

"Where were you before?" I asked, entering the kink in nature scene in front of me; shackles on trees, whips hanging from branches, benches near bushes, a cross with a reed fence, a portable shower, and chairs scattered everywhere. They had cordoned off areas, but it didn't seem like Craig wanted us to go there.

"We were in Gunnison National Forest in Colorado last year and next year we will be in Grand Canyon National Park. We only host events for three or four months a year and it's usually the most pleasant months. People want to be in nature with nice weather, not freeze their nipples off," he said with a smile.

They reminded me of a circus, but for kinky people. "As Officer Graham mentioned in the phone call, do you recall seeing this woman?" I asked, holding up a photo of Melissa.

"Can't say that I do," he said, reaching for the photo and shaking his head. "Nah, so many women look like her, if you know what I'm saying." He shrugged, handing me back the photo.

"Could we get a list of your employees?" I asked, placing the photo back into the folder. The newspaper clippings from last year were from Gunnison and this year it's happening in Sawtooth. If our killer was targeting women from the kink scene, and was in the same places as this show, then it was possible he was an employee of The Pleasure Zone.

"Yeah, sure," Craig said, pulling his cell phone out of his pocket and started tapping on it. A moment later, my cell pinged. "We haven't been doing this long, but those guys have been with us from the start."

"Thanks," I said, raising my cell in recognition. I forwarded the email to Officer Graham so he could look into that for me.

Officer Graham nodded in my direction.

"There isn't much else I can show you," Craig said, glancing around. "Just a whole lot of kink happens here and unfortunately I don't remember the girl—"

"What about her other name," I said, "Sensual Suzie."

Craig rubbed his chin with his index finger and thumb. "I don't know man, I don't sit at the door, nor do I interact with those taking part. My job is purely to arrange venues and events."

"Who interacts with the participants?" Officer Graham asked, taking an interest in the interview.

"Hey Carol," Craig yelled above our heads.

Officer Graham and I spun around at the same time to see a blond head come into view. I glanced wide eyed at Officer Graham, who shrugged. Neither of us had seen this office within the sign.

"Quit your yelling," Carol said, stomping down the metal stairs on the side of the metal entrance. "I only caught parts of the conversation," she said, approaching. "Who are you seeking?"

I handed her the photo. "Her name is Melissa King. We believe her kink name is Sensual Suzie. She may have other names, but we only know of the one."

"Yeah," Carol said, nodding. "I recognize her." She handed back the photo. "Give me a second. Let me fetch the list." Carol ran back up the spiral staircase and returned with a clipboard. She mumbled to herself as she scanned page after page. "Yep, she was here," Carol said, tapping the page, and showed it to me. "This is from our latest event."

I took the clipboard from her, and glanced at all the names on the list and who they attended with. Officer Graham moved around Carol to see. "Do you know who this is?" I asked, pointing at Sensual Suzie's plus one.

Carol glanced nervously up at Craig, who nodded. "Erik. He's one of our V.I.P Dominants," she said.

"Does he follow the events?"

"Yes," Carol said. "I've got his name and number."

"Before you get that," I said, needing more information. "Can you tell me about him?"

"He's been in the scene long before Craig. If I remember correctly, he suggested the idea of hosting these types of events to Craig—"

"That's right," Craig said. "We met when I still worked in Chicago. With my background in events management, he said it would be a good idea, and it was. We've grown quite a bit these last two years."

"Where can we find Erik?"

Carol ran upstairs again and returned, handing me a piece of paper with his details on.

"Thanks," I said. "If you remember anything else, here's my number." I handed a card each to Carol and Craig.

Chapter Ten

FRIEND OR FOE

Detective Steve Campbell

My vehicle rolled to a stop, and my jaw slackened at the view.

"Holy cow," Officer Graham said beside me. "What does this guy do for a living?"

"I don't know, but I'd like to find out." I opened my car door and stepped out onto the sidewalk. The large wrought-iron gate creaked open automatically, as if sensing our arrival. The cameras perched at various strategic places swiveled, following our movement. We stepped through the open side gate and once we were on the other side, the gate closed behind us.

Officer Graham knocked on the large wooden front door, but only managed one knock when a tiny woman with long silver hair yanked it open. She glowered up at us.

"Who you?" she asked with an Asian accent.

We introduced ourselves and asked to speak with Erik Cooper.

"Sir Cooper not available," she said, glancing over her shoulder and closed the door slightly. "Leave card and I get him to call back to you?"

"I'm afraid I can't do that," I said, stepping forward and placing my foot between the open door and the door frame. If she closed it on me, at least my foot could keep it open. All we wanted to do was ask him questions, yet this tiny woman's behavior left me feeling suspicious. "We're investigating a murder, and we need to speak with him."

The woman's eyes widened.

"Who is it, Esmeralda?" A man said from beyond the door. The tiny woman flinched, slamming the door onto my foot, but instead of it closing, it bounced off my foot and almost hit her in the face. A meaty hand grabbed the door, stopping it from hitting my foot again, and opened it wider. "Who are you?" The man demanded.

"Are you Erik Cooper?" I asked, removing my foot.

"Yes," Erik said. The lines between his brows deepening. His dark brown eyes bore holes into my face and the shift in his demeanor left me on edge, forcing me to rest my hand on my gun at my hip.

The small woman slunk away, giving Erik space to fill the door frame with his large, muscular body. The man worked out more than he should, and his thick neck strained against the collar of his white work shirt.

I introduced us and handed him my card. "We're here in connection with Melissa King's murder."

Erik's shoulders dropped, and he opened the door wider. "What happened to my Sensual Suzie?" he asked with concern etched in his tone. "Please come in." He stepped to one side, giving us access. "Esmeralda," he yelled. "Make my guests some coffee."

The silver-haired woman scurried across the neatly polished marble tiles and entered the kitchen while our host pointed us in the opposite direction.

We followed Erik into a lavish room that smelled like musk. He had lined the walls with floor to ceiling bookshelves, with a large wooden desk near the windows at the back, and two two-seater leather sofas in the center with a coffee table between them. The room reminded me of a library in a men's only club. Now all we needed were naked women, whiskey, and cigars.

"Please sit," Erik said, sitting on one of the leather sofas and gestured for us to sit across from him.

Esmeralda entered shortly thereafter, carrying a tray filled with mugs, a coffee pot, and a bowl of sugar cubes.

"Thanks, Esmeralda," Erik said. "Please help yourself to some coffee. Now tell me what has happened to my precious Melissa."

I explained to Erik what had happened and how we came across his name. He listened intently and cancelled his ringing phone three times. When I had finished, his cell phone rang a fourth time. He answered and instructed them to call back later.

"Please excuse the phone. Running my business from home never ends. And the news about Melissa is just terrible, awful," Erik said, finishing his coffee. He placed his mug on the table between us and leaned back. The man was enormous with his muscular body and tall frame, making the seat look miniature compared to him. "I was with her that evening. We met there, enjoyed the event, and then I left her there because I had a prior engagement back home." A sly grin stretched his face.

A door slammed somewhere in the house, followed by

footsteps running across the marble floors. Erik glanced above our heads, scowled, then quickly schooled his features. The footsteps neared. I glanced over my shoulder and caught sight of someone running barefoot through the hallway.

"Did either you or Melissa speak with anyone else at the event? Or did you notice someone wanting to speak with her?" I asked.

He shook his head. "No, I can't recall anyone else. I said hello to a few close friends, but none spoke with her. She was a lovely woman. I can't understand who would do such a thing." Erik looked sad. Almost.

"Where were you last night?"

The lines between Erik's brows creased. "Home," he retorted.

"Was there someone with you?"

"Of course, a few someone's." He white knuckled the armrests.

"We would like to speak with these someone's."

"Sure, they're around here somewhere," he said, grinning. I didn't know what he meant, and wouldn't leave until we spoke with whoever these people were.

"Can you think of anything else to tell us?"

Erik shook his head. "No," he said. His cell phone rang again, almost vibrating off the table. "I need to get this, or they won't stop." He stood, grabbed his cell, and stomped out of the room, and barked a *'what now'* as he exited.

Officer Graham stood and walked around the room with his hands behind his back, reminding me of Sherlock Holmes investigating a book thief.

I stood and joined him near a second door that seemed like an entrance or exit somewhere else. "What do you think?" I asked, leaning more to his side.

"Honestly," Officer Graham said, "I'm not sure. I think he's telling the truth, but he is hiding something."

"We'll need to look into him when we get back to the station," I said, peering through the gap of the door left ajar. I immediately pushed the door open all the way and entered the next room.

"Good grief," Officer Graham said behind me, taking the words right out of my mouth.

The air conditioner whirred overhead as it sent a blast of cold air near my face, making me shiver. The black leather straps reflected light, which was a stark contrast to the purple velvet couch. On either side of the white walls hung heavy-looking shackles and chains with a thick metal collar on the end, and on the walls were large portraits of naked women in various positions, with Erik in the middle, reminding me of a king.

The room also reminded me of The Play Spot & Anonymous Dungeon, but the only difference was there were women still here, who were naked, chained, and in various stages of excitement. We had interrupted Erik's play session.

Seeing these helpless women made me want to rescue them and free them from their chains, but they seemed quite happy to be attached to their Master's steel equipment.

"Sorry about that," Erik said behind me. "Your arrival came while we were in the middle of a very intense session," he chuckled.

"With three women?" I asked, my eyes bouncing across the naked bodies before me. I didn't want to look, but I couldn't tear my eyes away either.

"I was with these three ladies all night long. Wasn't I ladies?" Erik said.

"Yes, Master," the ladies said as one.

"This is Cassie," Erik said, standing beside a large busted, red-headed woman. They had surgically enlarged her breasts to the point where I'd need two hands just to cover one, and she had large nipple rings through each nipple and a chain connecting her nipples to a ring I could barely see between her legs.

"Amanda," Erik said, pointing at an Asian brunette. She seemed to be the smallest of the three. She was bound by her wrists and ankles, her arms and legs spread wide, leaving nothing to my imagination.

"And this is Liza," Erik pointed at a small-breasted blond who had her wrists tied to her ankles with everything on display.

Officer Graham shifted uncomfortably beside me.

"These ladies live with me. They work from home and are at my beck and call. They are my slaves, but the good kind of slave." He sounded pleased with himself. "And the little one running around in the hallway is my newest pet, and she enjoys getting spankings for disobeying her Master." He grinned.

"Willingly, I hope," I said, and the atmosphere shifted from a welcoming heat to an unpleasant cold.

"Of course, willingly," Erik said in anger. "I force no one to do something they don't want to do. I'm not into forcing myself onto anyone, Detective, and your insinuation is insulting." He was almost shouting, spit flying out of his mouth.

I raised my hands in mock surrender. "My apologies. I meant no disrespect, only ignorance. I've met no one who had three or four women living with him in this way. Everything is very new to me. Please forgive me."

Erik exhaled, closed his eyes, and nodded. “Come, if you have no more questions, I need to get back to my girls, and then my business.”

I took that as our cue to leave.

Chapter Eleven

RESEARCHING ERIK COOPER

Officer Graham

While investigating our previous case, Jack Haskins, and the disappearance of many women, we realized that someone had removed evidence relating to his parent's murder, and I took it upon myself to figure out who had done that. I had requested security footage of the evidence locker, but so far there was nothing I could use, and I was yet to find the footage of when the evidence actually went missing.

I sighed audibly and closed the email, then opened the search bar, typed in 'Erik Cooper', and links flooded my screen about the real estate tycoon. There were pictures of Erik standing beside celebrities, politicians, and billionaires. And from the various articles, there was no mention of Erik in any kink scene.

"What have you found?" Detective Campbell asked, sitting across from my desk.

"Erik rubs shoulders with the rich and famous, but there's nothing about him being kinky."

Detective Campbell arched an eyebrow.

"I know," I said, scanning more articles. "He brags about having slaves and pets in private, but out there it's all hidden. He comes across as an eligible bachelor."

"Can you blame him?"

"No, but still."

"He has a reputation to uphold," Detective Campbell said. "People like him won't just admit what they do in the bedroom. It's all done in secrecy and I'm sure they'll do everything to protect their secret."

"Yeah," I said. Although Detective Campbell was right, it didn't mean I had to like it.

"Any arrests?"

I shook my head, looking at our systems database. "Nothing. He's squeaky clean from the looks of it. Not even a traffic violation." I sounded as deflated as I felt. For the first time since starting this case, I felt stuck.

Detective Campbell rubbed his face. He looked tired, too. "What about the list from Craig?"

"Oh yes," I said, and opened the attachment. "There are ten males and two females; Carol and Mandy." I proceeded with a search of the women, which went quickly, then I started looking into the men. "The women are clean and I'm halfway through the list of men. The top five have nothing. Give me ten minutes to check the rest."

Detective Campbell nodded. "Give me two of the names and I'll check them."

"Okay." I read the two names, and he checked on his laptop while I searched on mine. "He has a record. Trevor Bishop for public indecency—"

"Jared Namar," Detective Campbell said, "DUI."

"Allen Hudson," I said, "assault."

"They're a bunch of upstanding citizens," Detective Campbell said sarcastically.

"Tell me about it," I said. "We'll need to find out whether they have any connections to our victim."

We fell silent as we each performed an in-depth search.

Twenty minutes later, Detective Campbell glanced up and massaged his neck. "I've found no connection to Melissa, but that doesn't mean one of them didn't speak with her considering they worked at The Pleasure Zone," he said, still rubbing his neck.

"I'll get a schedule from Craig to see when his guys worked and when Melissa attended The Pleasure Zone."

Detective Campbell nodded. "If that's the only connection we have, it's a start. We need to interview each of them. I'll set it up, ask them to come down to the station."

"Okay, or we can get some of our guys to go pick them up."

"Sounds good," Detective Campbell said. His phone vibrated, and he pulled it out of his shirt pocket. "Rachel Brink said we should stop by her office now that she's done with Melissa's autopsy," he said, reading the message on his cell phone.

"Now?" I asked.

"Yep," Detective Campbell said, glancing up. "I don't know about you, but I'm eager to hear what she found."

"Sure, and at least we get to hear all the gory details before dinner."

He grinned. "Luckily, and I was looking forward to Alice's meal." He stood up and headed for the exit.

I moved the cursor to close the articles when one woman Erik had his arm draped around caught my attention. I grabbed the copies of the newspaper clippings I'd found and smiled. Just when I thought things felt like we were going around in circles I made a connection. Erik knew one of the Gunnison victims.

Chapter Twelve

MELISSA REVEALED

Detective Steve Campbell

"I found a picture where Erik is holding one of the Gunnison victims," Officer Graham said, paling.

"He's in the kink scene and from the sounds of it, he meets up with a lot of women. Regardless, we can question him about it."

"Okay."

I shook my head. "We've been so busy with other leads we forgot to look into the four victims from Gunnison."

"I'll look into that next," Officer Graham said, standing beside me, swaying. Then he leaned against a gurney for stability.

"Are you okay?" I asked, knowing this wasn't his first time here.

"Yeah," he said, looking a little green around the edges. "One day I'm fine, the next time I'm here and it hits me." He shuddered.

"Maybe sit over there." I pointed at a lonely chair in the far corner of the cold, sterile basement.

Officer Graham didn't argue and headed for the chair as Rachel, our new coroner, entered, holding a heart in her gloved hand. Gagging sounded behind me, but I didn't look. I knew it was Officer Graham who had noticed the organ.

"Detective," Rachel said, smiling. "Just the cop I was waiting to see." She placed the heart onto a scale, wrote something down, then approached a wall lined with metal doors and opened one that was more or less in the middle, and pulled out a metal gurney holding Melissa's body.

Stepping closer, I stood on the other side of the metal gurney and swallowed hard. I'd attended many post-mortems before, yet each time I waited to hear the results, a sense of dread filled me from the pit of my stomach all the way to my chest. I exhaled, steadying my breathing, and felt better.

Rachel pointed at the bruises on Melissa's neck, across her chest, wrists, and ankles. "They strapped her down tightly, most likely restricting her movement and breathing," she said clinically, then she glanced up at me. "Are you familiar with B.D.S.M?"

"Yes, we've discovered she has been using an alias and has attended various dungeons for play sessions and kink events."

Rachel nodded her understanding. "She had old bruising that was most likely from her previous play session, but the fresh wounds were rough. It's something no submissive should ever agree to. It was harsh, and they meant to hurt her before strangling her." Rachel was quiet as she allowed her words to sink in, then cleared her throat. "They ripped open her one breast with a blunt tool," she said, pointing at the large incision. "And they sexually assaulted her with various objects."

Her words caught my attention and raised my brows.

"I'm uncertain what they used, but it was a metal object, and possibly something similar to a blade or sharp object."

"Jesus," I breathed, not believing it.

"When you told me about the other victims in the newspaper article, my assistant phoned Gunnison's coroner, and they had similar findings with their four victims."

Officer Graham groaned behind me; he seemed to struggle quite a bit today.

"Anything else?" I asked.

"She was already dead during the worst part of the torture. Which is a miracle. She suffocated to death when they obstructed her breathing. I suspect they had used a belt around her neck and a thick piece of leather around her chest and then possibly sitting on top of her." She pointed at the various bruises on her chest.

"And the women in Gunnison?"

"Same," she said. "They all died similar ways. Some had knife wounds across their backs, others had the outer labia sewn together, which were then savagely torn open with an object. Whoever is doing this is torturing these women for their sick pleasure."

"And the pieces of flesh cut out of Melissa?"

"That too," Rachel said. "The killer cuts two pieces of flesh in the shape of a leaf from their backs." A sadness I hadn't noticed before was evident on her face and I wondered if this was the worst case Rachel had worked on, because it certainly was mine.

"Were you able to find any traces of his D.N.A?"

"No, nothing, and the Gunnison coroner also found nothing."

"Thanks, Rachel, I appreciate the feedback."

"This happened to four women in Gunnison," Rachel said. "Do we know if this is his first victim in the Sawtooth Forest or are there others?"

Chapter Thirteen

INTERVIEW SUSPECTS

Detective Steve Campbell

After meeting with Rachel, I desperately wanted to get back to Sawtooth Forest to widen the search using cadaver dogs. But before we could do that, officers picked up the three men and brought them to the station to be interviewed. Officer Graham was interviewing Trevor Bishop, arrested for public indecency. Officer Crick was interviewing Jared Namar, DUI, while I had the pleasure of interviewing Allen Hudson; arrested for assault.

"Do you know this woman?" I asked, producing a picture of Melissa in front of him.

Allen picked up the photo and licked his lips. "She sure is pretty," he said, smiling. He was missing a top front tooth, and the rest of his teeth were rotten and stained. Sweat peppered his oily skin and his t-shirt had black stains on the sleeves. "What happened to her?"

"She's dead."

"'Ain't me," Allen said, raising both hands. His hands were rough and stained, with scrapes from working on car engines.

"Do you work at The Pleasure Zone?"

"Yes, sir, I do. But I'm only there in the mornings to help set up the equipment, then I go to my other job. I don't hang around with those weird people." He visibly shuddered. "Have you seen what those perverts do? It's gross man. A man and a woman belong together and do normal stuff. What those folk do," he shook his head, "is against God."

"Are you a religious man?"

"Yes, sir, and been married fifteen years."

"Who is your wife?"

"The same woman who accused me of assault that got me arrested."

"Why did she press charges?"

"We had a fight, and she accused me of cheating on her. Which I didn't. She angered me and I hit her a little too hard, but I apologized, and she forgave me." He raised his hands in prayer. "We started attending church after that day and have been going ever since. I stopped drinking and I make an honest living working two to three jobs."

I sighed internally. Allen looked like scum, but in this job, looks were deceiving.

"I'm sorry that girl is dead, but it wasn't me. She sure is pretty though, but not as pretty as my lady."

I ended the interview and listened in on Officer Graham's interview, which was going much the same as mine. Officer Crick's interview had lasted five minutes; Jared Namar was working in Alaska and returned yesterday morning. He provided proof.

None of the men recognized Melissa and had only taken part in the setup of the various scenes. We had to let them go, but not before getting their details and where we could find them if we needed them again.

Chapter Fourteen

CADAVER DOGS

Detective Steve Campbell

The interviews with the men felt like a setback and we lost time, but that didn't matter. We were back at Sawtooth Forest hiking trail near Bald Mountain to see if there were other victims we may have missed. I hated we were doing this in the first place because I didn't want there to be more victims, but the possibility of there being another body could help our chances of finding more evidence and who the killer was.

Two men waited for us at the mouth of the hiking trail, each with a dog sitting obediently beside them.

"Thank you for coming at such short notice," I said, shaking their hands.

"No problem," Kellen said. "This is Duke," he nodded at the Belgian Malinois.

"Happy to help," Mitch said, "and this is Mabel." He rubbed Mabel on her head, she was a Bloodhound.

I smiled. "Great, let them do their thing."

Kellen and Mitch unhooked their dog's leashes and said a command. Immediately, their dogs reacted and ran into the forest with their handlers and us running after them.

At first Duke and Mabel ran together, sniffing the air, then they separated. It was as if they had arranged who would go where and went in that direction.

"Follow Duke," I said to Officer Graham while I followed Mabel.

Officer Graham did as I asked and ran after Duke. His gait seemed a little off, like he had a hip injury, but I suspected it was just the uneven ground.

Mabel headed off the hiking trail, darted through bushes, between trees until she finally stopped. She whined near a tree with roots growing out of the ground. Kellen stopped beside me and snapped the leash back onto her collar.

"Good dog," Kellen said, rubbing her head. "You all good here?" he asked me.

"Yeah," I said sadly.

"We can walk around to see if we can find anything else but Mabel isn't acting like there could be something else."

"That's okay, I think this is it," I said. And the way Duke had gone off I suspected they, too, would find something. "And thanks." I watched Kellen and Mabel amble back, and I pulled out my phone to call Rachel.

"It looks like the roots were protecting them," Officer Graham said.

"Or keeping them down," I added, rubbing my tired face.

We stood near the third grave; the one Officer Graham

had found with Duke. It was the farthest crime scene from the first and this victim was in worse condition. She was naked, sitting in an upright position, her hands palm side up and resting on her thighs, and her cloudy eyes stared blankly ahead of her. An animal had gotten to her and had torn pieces of her flesh from her bones. But the weirdest part about these scenes were the roots of the large trees intertwined in and around their bodies as if covering them.

James approached and kneeled beside her. “I agree with Rachel,” he started, “this is one of the weirdest crime scenes I’ve ever been to. I mean, just look at this,” he said, gesturing at the roots.

The Sawtooth Forest had a variety of fir trees, but there were also a variety of trees where the roots grew above ground.

“I know we’ve been busy with leads sending us to dungeons, events, and personal homes, but when you get back to the office, can you speak with Gunnison Police and compare notes,” I said, and Officer Graham scribbled in his notebook. “Find out what trees were the women found near? What level of decay were they found in? Which victim was first and was their experience similar to ours? And who did they suspect? We must get as much information from them as possible.”

“Okay,” he said, nodding and scribbling. “I think I’m going to head on out now to do this. You’re good here?” he asked.

“I’m fine, thanks,” I said, glancing down at the victim.

Once Officer Graham was out of sight, I turned to James. “I’ll be right back,” I said and traversed the path as I headed in the direction of the next victim.

Victim number two was the only one with her face in

the mud. They would need to be careful to scrape the mud off her body to check for any D.N.A.

Rachel moved her onto her back and I noted her bright red hair and gray eyes.

"Do you think they all died the same way?" I asked, crouching near the victim's right hand.

"Yeah," Rachel said, sounding exhausted. "They all present with similar bruising, and I can only imagine the rest." She pointed at the victim's destroyed breast, much like the other two. "It will take us a while to do their autopsies, but you'll find out what happened to them as soon as possible." She filled her tone with determination, which left me feeling slightly better. "What's this killer's name?"

"We haven't really thought of it. BTK is already taken," I said. "Kinky Killer, maybe," I said, raising a shoulder.

"I guess it doesn't matter, just as long as you get him."

And get him we would. I hated that this killer had tortured and killed these women, then dumped them here, putting their bodies on display like they were nothing. Sometimes I hated my job; and today was one of those times.

"I'll be back now," I said, pointing toward the area where we had found the first victim and headed that way.

The distance from the first victim to the second and then third was all within a mile of each other. It was times like these I wished there were cameras in and around the forest so that we had filmed him; our life would be so much easier.

There were still markers on the ground where Melissa's body had been and, from a quick glance, nothing much had changed. I headed back to the cave where we had found the shrine and newspaper clippings. Before, there was no path to the cave, but now I saw a distinct path from us gathering evidence and returning to ensure we had missed nothing.

I entered the cave and breathed in the smell of damp soil. We had cleared the shrine area, leaving nothing but the wet rock and small droplets falling from the cave ceiling and splashing onto the surface. The wind blew through the trees, creating a hypnotic sound that, on any other day, I would appreciate, but not today. When leaves rustled and a twig snapped, I spun around in time to see something black blur past. My heart thundered in my chest, and I kicked off after him.

I reached the edge of the cave opening and went in the direction they had gone. I ran after them, pushing branches out of my face, and ran until my lungs burned. The sound of their footsteps stopped, and I stopped, searching for movement, but soon realized there was nothing out there.

I hadn't imagined someone there, I thought as I wiped beads of sweat from my forehead and stood still as I surveyed my surroundings. It wasn't my imagination. My mind never played tricks on me like this. Someone had been there, but now… nothing.

Chapter Fifteen

GUNNISON GIRLS

Officer Graham

"Morning," I said into the receiver. "I'm Officer Graham from Ketchum Police Station, and I'd like to speak with the person in charge involving the four women found in Gunnison Forest."

"Morning, okay, please hold," a woman said on the other line. A beep sounded and then a click, followed by a shuffling of papers and a clank.

"Hi," a woman said. *"Who are you?"*

"I'm Officer Graham from Ketchum Police Station, and I'd like to speak with the person in charge involving the four women found in Gunnison Forest," I repeated.

"It's one of the worst cases I've ever worked on," she said. *"I'm Detective Blayne, by the way. What do you need?"*

"It seems the killer has moved down to Sawtooth Forest in Idaho." It sounded like she gasped on the other end. "And I was hoping you could share some information you may have that could help us."

"Yes, of course," she said and started tapping on her keyboard. *"One similarity was they were all recently divorced, no current boyfriend and no kids. And I'm sure you've realized it has a B.D.S.M component."*

"Yes, we've made that connection, too," I said.

"They were all bound so tightly they would've suffocated if he didn't strangle them. There were lots of bruises, mutilations, and then raped with various objects. Our coroner had mentioned the killer had scrambled their cervix and womb. It's just terrible what he did to them."

I swore under my breath upon hearing this and felt sorry for the women.

"Did you have any suspects?" I asked, swallowing hard.

"We had one suspect who managed the B.D.S.M event, but he had video recordings as an alibi, along with multiple witnesses. One suspect was a play partner, but was quickly ruled out when he produced an alibi for each of the murders. Otherwise no, nobody."

"Can you think of anything else that may help us?"

"Let me go through the cases again and I'll get back to you. Give me your number."

I gave her my number, and she promised to get back to me in a day or two. I hoped we had that much time and the killer wasn't planning on a fifth victim.

Chapter Sixteen

DARBY IN CHAINS

The Dominant

Darby tested her restraints, but they were so tight she barely had any wriggle room. "Orange, Daddy," she breathed through the ball gag in her mouth, saliva dripping down her chin and onto her naked breasts.

The dominant smiled approvingly at the words *"Daddy's Cunt"* written in black pen across her naked chest.

"Orange, Daddy… Sir," Darby said again, sucking in a breath.

The dominant rubbed coconut oil all over his naked muscular body, his fingers brushing lightly against his tattoos, all the while staring deeply into Darby's green eyes. "You like this, don't you, little one?" he said gruffly.

Darby nodded, her eyes rolling into the back of her head the moment he pressed the Hitachi Magic Wand against her pussy, sending wave upon wave of pleasure straight to her core.

"Yeah, you do like that." He grinned and removed the Hitachi Magic Wand.

Darby's eyes shot open.

"Don't worry," he said, scooping more coconut oil in his hand and pressing it against her already wet core. "But first, I need to make sure you stay wet. I can't have my Darby in Chains getting hurt."

The dominant continued his pleasurable assault on Darby's body by pressing the Wand against her pussy and removing it just before she came. Edging his submissive play partner was something all dominant's enjoyed doing; the overwhelming feeling of holding her orgasms in his hands. That only he could give her the pleasure she so desperately wanted and needed and would do anything to get it. Then, when the time finally arrived, and she was dripping with desperation, he gave her what she wanted.

When Darby's eyes rolled into the back of her head as her orgasms smashed into her one after the other until finally her subspace engulfed her, the dominant knew it was time to stop. They had agreed on certain things before their play session and he would never take advantage of her, not when she was in such a vulnerable state.

The dominant freed Darby of her restraints and helped her walk from the bench to the soft bed. He carefully helped her onto the satin sheets and, as she curled into the fetal position, he climbed in behind her, wrapping his powerful arms tightly around her.

The dominant breathed in deeply and exhaled as his submissive continued floating in her sub-high. He had heard how powerful it could be for some submissive's, that it was akin to taking a blissful drug. That all those feel-good hormones rushed in her veins, sending her to a magical place where only she could go.

He got to enjoy his own version of subspace; Dom-space or Dominant-high, which he received purely from watching her enjoy herself. His pleasure was making her smile and giving her the ecstasy she deserved.

What woman didn't want a powerful orgasm that could last minutes?

The dominant breathed in deeply once more, noting his little submissive was breathing deeply, too. He smiled. He brushed some hair out of her face, and she stirred, a lazy smile crossing her exhausted face.

"How do you feel?" he asked, gently planting a kiss on her cheek.

"Thank you, Sir I mean Daddy, that was," she said, licking dry lips, "something I'd never experienced before." She licked her lips again. "It was magical, euphoric, divine, and oh, so pleasurable." She continued smiling but kept her eyes closed.

"I'm glad you enjoyed it, little one." He sat up. "And you can call me Sir or Daddy, I don't mind."

"It feels strange calling you, Daddy, you know, considering we're almost the same age."

He chuckled. "Don't stress about it. Sir is perfect, too." He enjoyed it when a submissive called him by either title; it gave him an edge of power and dominance over her. Having a title ensured they each played their role during the play session. He would never abuse the power exchange, no matter what his submissive called him.

He reached for the bottle of water that had electrolytes in. "Drink."

He helped her sit up, her eyes opening slowly, and she took the bottle from him.

"Thank you, Sir," she said and drank. When she swallowed the first bit of water, it fueled her thirst and she gulped more down, not breathing.

"Easy, Darby, I don't want you choking. I mean, I want you choking on my cock, but never water," he said, chuckling.

Darby grinned and slowed down. Her eyes focused on him and his cock jumped. She had the prettiest green eyes he'd ever seen and a gorgeous smile to match it.

"Was everything fine?" he asked, wanting to make sure he didn't hurt her during their first play session.

"Yes, Sir, it was more than I had ever hoped for. More than I'd ever read about. I'd never experienced a sub-high before and that, dear kind Sir, was delicious. And I hope Sir will do it again for me."

"Good," he said, nodding. The last thing he wanted was an unhappy submissive. "And I will absolutely play with you again. Just let me know when." He kissed her cheek. "I hate to leave, but are you okay if I do? I have a business meeting this afternoon and need to get ready." He rarely had a morning play session, but he and Darby had hit it off after months of online chatting. He wanted to meet and play with her, and this was the only time she had available.

"Yeah," she said, nodding. "I'm going to have a shower," she glanced at the open shower in the opposite corner, "and then head off to an early dinner with my friend."

"Enjoy dinner and we can continue our chat online?"

"Yes, please, Sir. I'd like that very much."

Darby slipped her boots on, fixed her jean jacket, and applied some makeup. While she smacked her dark red lips together, she didn't hear the side door opening and closing.

Darby didn't notice the figure sticking to the dark shadows as he neared. And she didn't feel his presence as he came up behind her, even though she stood in front of the mirror. Darby was too busy digging in her handbag to stop the man from collaring her with his leather belt.

And since Darby had booked this dungeon for the entire day, there would be nobody needing to enter the venue after her. Therefore, nobody would hear her painful screams.

Chapter Seventeen

VICTIM #4

Detective Steve Campbell

My phone screamed early the next morning, forcing me to smack it away, instead, I hit the bedside table, hurting my wrist. I grumbled and moaned as I sat up and finally answered my phone.

"Hello?" I said, rubbing my eyes, yawning.

"Detective," Officer Graham said in a panicked tone. *"We have another victim."* He waited for my reply, but I was too gobsmacked to utter a word. *"He dumped her sometime last night. One of Rachel's assistants went back to the crime scene this morning for another soil sample when he stumbled upon the new crime scene."*

"Dammit," I said, scratching the back of my head. "Are you there now?"

"I'm on my way now only."

"Can you pick me up?"

"See you soon."

Officer Graham arrived at the same time I exited my

house. Alice kissed my cheek and closed the door behind me.

"Talk about a morning wake up call," I said as I sat in the passenger seat and closed the car door. "What else do we know?"

"Morning," Officer Graham said in a tone I'd never heard before. I was about to ask what was wrong when he continued speaking. "The victim's name is Darby Trent. She's thirty-three years old, never married, no kids, and no family. And from the description Rachel's assistant gave, I'd say it's the same killer."

"Everything else okay?" I asked, grabbing the door to keep from falling over when Officer Graham took a corner too fast.

Officer Graham sighed audibly and slowed the car. "Sorry," he said, shaking his head. "I've been trying to get to the bottom of who removed the evidence from our last case and I'm just hitting walls."

"Don't worry about it. Whoever did it will reveal themselves soon. Things like that always come out. So, for now, let's rather focus on what we can control, like this case."

Officer Graham nodded and glanced quickly my way. "You're right. I'll leave the probing for a while until I have more time to give it the attention it needs."

I stepped over another tree with roots growing out of the ground, its woody crooked fingers reaching for my ankles. I crossed the hiking path and down a slope, careful not to slip. During the night we had some rain, leaving everything wet and most likely had washed away all D.N.A traces.

I reached the latest victim, who was a brunette. They

had already placed her in a body bag to preserve the D.N.A that was left.

"Apparently, she was sitting in an upright position when found," I said.

"Yep," James said, "he had covered her in mud, leaves, and broken branches, like he was trying to hide her." He stood up to stretch his back. "I've been at this since early this morning." He glanced down at the slope. "Don't you find it strange that she's the only one on the other side of the hiking trail?"

"Yes, it's strange. Then again, who knows what goes on in this killer's mind?" Standing quietly, I closed my eyes and took in my surroundings; insects, birds, wind, and the sound of moving water. It was much quieter here than on the other side; which seemed to have more wind, more rustling, just more of everything. "Perhaps the killer enjoyed the calmness that was here. Apart from her crime scene, it's lovely on this side of the mountain."

"It is lovely here," James said, glancing around. "It's also closest to the parking area. Maybe the killer didn't have time to find a more secluded spot."

"It's possible," I said. "Any feedback on the other girls?"

"We have their names."

"Well, don't leave me in suspense."

"The redhead is Rebecca Crown. She was the one who was the most decomposed. She got divorced a year ago and her brother is on his way to identify her body. The other brunette is Brianna Woods, she had the animal bite marks. We think it was a red fox. Brianna's dad is on his way to identify her."

It relieved me we now had their names, but it didn't make my job any easier. "Do you know the times their family members are arriving?"

James glanced at his watch. "They should be there in an hour."

"Anything else you can tell me about Darby?"

James stopped bagging evidence and stood up. "She's petite compared to the other ladies. At first glance, it appears she has more bruises than the others. They tore hair and skin out of her head, and they hit her in the face a few times before strangling her. I may be wrong, but this seemed personal while the others were just kills for this guy." He shrugged nonchalantly and continued with his job.

"Thanks, James, that helps more than you know. Let me know if you find something else. I'm going to head back to the morgue to speak with the deceased family members."

"Good luck," James said solemnly. "It's going to be a rough day."

I traversed the path back toward the car, but before I exited, I found Officer Graham digging in the dirt near the area where we'd found Melissa.

"You lose something?" I asked.

"Just looking," he said, dusting his hands. "I thought I saw something, but there's nothing." He stood up.

"Did you find anything at the other scenes?" I'd asked Officer Graham to double check the areas where we found the other victims.

"No, there's nothing else," he said, dusting sand off his hands. "Are we heading out?"

"Yeah, I want to speak with the family members arriving at the morgue to identify their loved ones."

Chapter Eighteen

THE OTHER GIRLS

Detective Steve Campbell

Officer Graham and I entered the morgue where Rachel and two assistants waited, each standing beside a victim of Sawtooth Forest.

"Have you been waiting long?" I asked, approaching Rachel while Officer Graham stood beside me. I had phoned from the road asking whether she was done with the autopsies and if she could go through her findings with us before the family members arrived.

"We just finished completing a few things before you arrived," Rachel said without smiling. "We must be quick, though. Their families are on their way."

"Okay, let's hear it," I said, standing so that I could see all three victims.

"I've already gone over Melissa's autopsy with you," Rachel said, pointing at the body on the gurney in front of her, "so I won't do that again. We're waiting for James to bring Darby in but I asked him to wait half an hour before leaving so that it gives us time with the family. The last thing I want is for them to see another victim being wheeled in." She shuddered.

Officer Graham fidgeted beside me. I gave him a sideways glance, but he didn't notice me.

My attention went back to the two assistants who uncovered the other two victims.

"This is Rebecca Crown," Rachel pointed at the gurney on her right, "she's forty-three years old, divorced for over a year, no children. I suspect she was the first victim because of how badly she had decomposed." Then she pointed to her left. "This is Brianna Woods, forty-eight, recently divorced. Her kids are adults and are out of the house. As you can see, we suspect a red fox bit off some parts of her abdomen and arms. And based on her decomposition, she was the second victim, with Melissa third, and now Darby being our latest."

Rachel instructed her assistants to cover the women and continued speaking. "The killer had abused and tortured all three women in similar ways. They were bound so tightly it cut off air supply, but it didn't kill them, but it did leave them in a constant state of semi-consciousness. He had whipped, lashed, cut, and raped them with various objects. He then strangled them repeatedly until finally they passed away. In all three, our killer then continued to stab their corpses and then raped them again with objects that cut."

Goosebumps spread across my shoulders, arms, and back, just imagining what these poor women had gone through. It relieved me they were already dead for the worse parts.

Officer Graham swayed slightly, but I was proud of him for staying on his feet.

"Was any D.N.A left behind?" I asked.

Rachel shook her head. "No, he must have used gloves, and we sent the traces we did find for processing. We'll know more next week."

"Okay, thanks, Rachel."

A knock on the door behind me made me flinch, and I spun around. The receptionist entered, her face red, while her eyes darted around.

"The families are here, Doctor," she said. She had to have been the new temp to assist Rachel. Her eyes flicked to me, then back to Rachel, and her cheeks flushed.

"Thanks Emily, show them to the waiting area and offer them coffee or tea. I'll be out in a minute while we make the arrangements for separate viewing."

"Sure, Doctor," Emily said, and closed the door behind her, but not before glancing my way again.

I turned back to see Officer Graham's cheeks were redder than before, and I wondered if she was staring at him instead of me. I smiled knowingly but was also curious; Officer Graham was a married man.

"I've asked Officer Crick to search the last place Darby had been, so perhaps we should go back to the station and find out?" Officer Graham said.

"I first want to speak with the family," I said.

Brianna Woods' father stood tall with a large belly hanging over his pants. His face was red, eyes were bloodshot, and he carried a handkerchief to wipe his tears. He was about to identify Brianna when I stopped him, introduced myself, and asked if he knew of anyone who would hurt her.

"No," Paul Woods said. "Brianna rarely visited me after her divorce. Her kids pop around more often than she does, but you know how it goes. Some people struggle to come to terms when things end."

"Do you know why they divorced?" I asked.

"They just grew apart." He shrugged, glancing down, and wiped another tear. "Soon after her divorce, she changed her last name back to Woods. Her ex Teddie Monroe moved to Colorado, and I saw her less and less. Her two daughters barely saw her." As he said that, two women entered the hallway. When they saw Paul, they ran to his open arms. The three of them cried their hellos, wiping their tears.

Once they had finished, they separated, and Paul introduced me. "Girls, this is Detective Campbell, Detective, this is Jana," he pointed at the youngest, "and this is Jane."

"Hi," I said. I opened my mouth to ask them a question when Paul asked it for me.

"He's looking into your mom's murder. Do either of you know who could've done this?"

Both girls shook their heads. Jana looked me in the eye and said 'no', while Jane glanced away.

"Jane," I said, stepping closer to her. "Do you have any information that could assist us?"

Jane looked up and something flickered in her eyes, then she stared at her grandfather.

"What is it, Jane?" Paul asked, reaching for her. "If you know anything, now is the time. We have to find the bastard who did this to your mom."

Jane nodded and turned to me. "This may tarnish Mom's reputation, but," she looked at her grandfather again, "it may help."

"It's okay, child. Tell him," Paul said reassuringly.

"Mom visited me soon after the divorce from Dad, then had to go. Normally, I wouldn't think anything of it, but the text message she had received seemed to have made her uncomfortable. She read the message, went to the bathroom, then hurried off. I wasn't sure what was going on, but before she left, I glanced at her phone and saw the message," Jane said, sighing audibly.

"Go on," Paul said. "It's okay. Whatever you share here is between us," Paul added, glancing at me.

"Absolutely. It will help our investigation," I said.

Jane glanced at Paul, then at me. "It was from a man named Monsieur." She swallowed hard. "He told her to go to the bathroom and remove her panties, and then meet him at some dungeon. I don't know what all that meant, and I never asked her about it. Whatever it was, was strange, and it stuck with me."

I nodded. We had already known a 'Monsieur' had met with Melissa and it seemed he met with Brianna, too. The command he had given her was because of the Dominant and submissive dynamic they had going on where he would tell her what to do and she would comply, no questions asked. It usually involved her doing something sexual and, in turn, excite him. These last couple of evenings I had been reading up on Dom/sub dynamics and the various things they would do; I still didn't fully understand why, but I was slowly starting to.

"Thanks, Jane," I said. "We will try to get her phone records and find out who Monsieur is."

Officer Graham scribbled notes in his book.

"When was the last time you saw your mom?"

"About a month ago," Jane said, and Paul nodded his agreement. We needed to establish a timeline of the last time she was seen and when she was murdered.

"Did that happen often?"

"Yeah," Jane said. "Sometimes we didn't see her for two

months at a time." It would explain why they didn't report her missing.

"If there's anything else you can think of, please let me know." I handed a business card to each of them and allowed one of Rachel's assistants to take them in to identify Brianna.

Rebecca Crown's brother stared at his sister's body through the glass window. He had the option of going inside but refused.

Rachel's assistant removed the sheet enough to show the part of her face that was the most presentable.

"Yeah," Reese said, glancing away. "That's her all right." He swallowed hard, then sucked in a deep breath. He blinked back tears and stood tall. "Is it okay if I leave? I need to prepare for her funeral."

"Before you go," I said, standing closer, "can you tell me if you know of anyone who would hurt her?"

"Try her useless ex-husband."

"Why do you say that?"

"He wanted to divorce her. When she showed him the prenup, which left him with nothing if he divorced her, he threatened to kill her."

"Can you give us his details?"

"Yeah, sure," Reese said, taking his phone out and read out Ivan Thompson's details. "Luckily, I ensured she changed her will to exclude him."

"Was your sister wealthy?" I asked.

"Our family has a large trust fund," Reese said, glancing nervously around. "And within the trust, we each have a substantial amount of money."

"Where would her portion of the money go now that her ex is out of the picture?"

"Back into the trust."

"So, the family would benefit."

"Yes, and if you think I or anyone in our family did this, you're gravely mistaken. We have more than enough money for ourselves. We don't need anybody else's."

I raised my hands in mock surrender. "I'm just doing my job and therefore need to ask these uncomfortable questions. We will contact Ivan and ask him to come in for an interview. And besides, Ivan, can you think of anything else? Did your sister attend any strange functions or places?"

Reese's eyebrows knitted together. "What do you mean? Rebecca was an upstanding member of the community and would never tarnish her reputation or that of her family. And if she did, we know nothing about it."

"How many are part of the trust?" I asked.

"About sixteen," he said. "Our great-great-great-grandfather made his money from oil; therefore we have a lifetime guarantee our trust will never run dry."

"Would you be willing to share who is part of that trust?"

Reese nodded. "I will check with our lawyer and get back to you."

"Thank you," I said. "You're welcome to ask your lawyer to call me. Here's my card." I handed it to him. "Before you go, do you know of a man named Monsieur interacting with your sister?"

Reese shook his head. "No, who is he?"

"That's what we want to find out," I said. "When was the last time you saw your sister?"

"About a month ago," Reese said, shrugging. "Or maybe more."

"And you didn't report her missing?"

"I didn't know she was missing until I received the call to identify her body," he said sadly.

"If you think of anything else, please let me know."

Reese pocketed my card and hurried out the door.

"He's on edge," Officer Graham said.

"Yeah," I said, "or maybe that's just how he handles grief. We all handle it in different ways."

Chapter Nineteen

DARBY - ABOUT LAST NIGHT

Detective Steve Campbell

We stood near Officer Crick's desk as he typed. He brushed his black hair out of his brown-colored eyes. "I got her credit card information for the last month," he said. "I browsed the statement, and she attended an event at The Pleasure Zone and at that dungeon you went to," Officer Crick said, glancing at me.

"The Play Spot & Anonymous Dungeon?" I asked.

"Yep, and I checked The Pleasure Zone line up. They have another event tonight," Officer Crick said, glancing from Officer Graham to me. "Perhaps we need to check it out?"

I had a sneaky suspicion Officer Crick had an affinity for these types of events, but we would need everybody to assist if we were to catch this guy. Not that we knew who to look for or who his next victim was.

I rubbed my face. "We need to speak with Craig Williams about the other victims. I'll inform Detective

Marshall from Boise. Perhaps he could bring some of his officers along to assist."

Officer Crick grinned. "I also got credit card statements for Brianna Woods and Rebecca Crown. I haven't gone through them yet. Perhaps we could sit in one of the conference rooms and review them?"

We sat around the conference room table with our late takeout lunches. I forked a piece of my Kung Pao chicken and flicked to the next page; it amazed me Rebecca could spend so much just in one month. If I had a limitless budget, I doubted I could spend half as much.

Officer Crick had gotten her statements from the day she divorced her husband, Ivan Thompson, a year ago. We got hold of Ivan and he produced a credible alibi and that he hadn't left Canada since after the divorce.

My finger traced the various charges; expensive dinners, expensive shoes, even more expensive handbags, and she travelled to Europe at least once a month for a four-day getaway. Rich people's problems.

Then, about five months ago, I came across a charge for The Pleasure Zone and a week later, another one for The Play Spot & Anonymous Dungeon. As I scanned the charges, the next month the same two charges came up for The Pleasure Zone and again a week later, another one for The Play Spot & Anonymous Dungeon. For the last four months on the first Friday of the new month, Rebecca attended an event and then she had a play session. She had no charges up until three weeks ago. I said as much to Officer's Graham and Crick.

Officer Graham nodded. "Brianna has something similar," he said, waving her statements in his hand. "These sessions weren't cheap, either. I mean, who can afford a two-hundred-and fifty-dollars full day play session every month when their salary is two-thousand."

"Rebecca has a limitless budget," I added.

Officer Crick whistled. "Melissa and Darby were every second month. Their budgets were quite a bit less. Melissa was in marketing and Darby worked in retail."

"Brianna was an accountant and owned her own company."

I rubbed my forehead. "Are there no other strange charges to their credit cards?" I asked, picking up the statement again. I turned the page, forked a piece of chicken into my mouth, and glanced at the various lines. "Does anyone know what 'Conquin' is? There's a charge here for seven-hundred and fifty dollars. I've never heard of such a place."

"Let me check," Officer Graham said, tapping away on his laptop.

"Melissa and Darby both have a charge for that on the same day two months ago."

"Yeah," I said, "Rebecca too. The sixth?"

"Yep," Officer Crick said. "What happened on the sixth?"

"The only thing I could find on 'Conquin' is a fancy mansion," Officer Graham said. "The site reveals nothing but a black screen and the words; *"If you would take, you must first give. This is the beginning of intelligence."* — Lao Tzu. Followed by '*Let us take you there…*' Then at the bottom there's a big button with the word '*Enter*'." He turned his laptop so we could see the black page with the words written in silver.

"Where are they so we can pay them a visit?"

"Boise," Officer Graham said, "and they're only open once a month for the weekend, and that is from tomorrow until Sunday."

"Does it say who owns the place?" I asked.

"Nope," Officer Graham said. "There's no mention of an owner or manager."

"I'll contact Detective Marshall," I said, pulling out my cell phone. "I'm sure he'll want to accompany us."

Chapter Twenty

A QUIET DINNER BEFORE THE CHAOS

Detective Steve Campbell

I sat at the dining table and sipped some water. Alice sat beside me, placing the napkin on her lap. She smiled, her eyes twinkling with life.

"You have a good day?" I asked, picking up my fork and scooping some mac and cheese.

"Yep," she said, chewing and swallowing. "I found a recipe for this dish and thought I'd try it."

"It tastes different. Is that rosemary?"

She nodded excitedly. "Yep, with salt and black pepper."

We ate in silence. I was yet to tell her I needed to go out tonight. She didn't know what kind of case I was working on and I was unsure how she would take the news. The last thing we needed now was her becoming insecure because of my job.

The silence between us seemed to stretch and pull as I thought of what to say. Everything I thought of sounded stupid. '*Ah, honey, I need to go to a kinky event tonight to find a killer we have no way of identifying,'* or *'this case I'm working on requires we attend this event...'* It was all dumb. Or I could just tell her it's a stakeout and leave it at that.

"Steve?" Alice said, staring at me with concern.

"What's wrong?" I asked, setting my fork down and giving her my attention.

"Where did you go to just now? I've been talking about our neighbor, Olivia, and you haven't heard a word."

"I'm sorry."

"What's going on? Is it this case you're busy with?"

"Yeah, I've been trying to figure out how to tell you I need to go out tonight. There's this event and I don't know what we're looking for, only that we need to go check it out."

She patted my hand and squeezed it. "It's okay. I know you want to protect me and you can't really talk about your cases. And wherever you need to go, I trust you." Her smile warmed my heart. I reached for her hand, bringing it to my lips, and kissed the top gently.

"I love you," I said.

"I love you, too," she said. "Ready for dessert?"

"Absolutely," I said, glancing at the clock on the wall across from me. I had forty minutes left and then I had to go.

"There's an old movie I'll watch and then I'll probably fall asleep. I hope you don't mind that I won't be waiting up for you."

"Not at all."

And I would do everything to leave that event as soon as possible so that I could spend the rest of my evening with my wife.

Chapter Twenty-One

AN EVENT ONE SHOULD MISS

Officer Graham

I shut off the engine and opened the window. The evening air was cool with hints of the night coming alive as people rushed off from work to stop at the shop or restaurant to get what they needed before going home.

"Not sure why you want to meet here," Officer Crick said, closing the gap. "I could've given this to you at the office." He leaned his elbows on the window frame with his face close to mine. I could smell his rancid breath and twisted my body in such a way I didn't smell it. "Cute pink bunny," he said, glancing at Stacey's plush toy she kept in my personal vehicle.

"Show me the video," I said, not in the mood for his banter.

Officer Crick stood back and pulled a bag from behind his back to his front and zipped it open. "Here," he said, handing me the device.

I pressed play and watched how someone dressed in

black entered the evidence locker and headed straight to the back where we kept Jack's parent's evidence box. The camera shifted to the next scene as it followed the man in a black walk down the aisle and then stood in front of the box. He reached in and removed D.N.A. samples.

I squinted at the device, trying to see if I recognized this person by the way they walked, but I saw no similarities. The camera shifted again as it followed the man to the exit of the evidence locker. He closed the gate behind him and then disappeared.

"Where's the rest of the footage? We had cameras in the precinct back then so we can see where he goes next."

"Unfortunately, we destroyed those tapes," Officer Crick shrugged nonchalantly. "Getting this took me forever. At least it's something."

"Can you recognize this person's gait or mannerisms?"

"Nothing, Officer Graham, that person could be any of us." He leaned forward again, almost sticking his head inside the window. "Now where's my '*thank you*'?"

I rolled my eyes and handed him a bag of chocolates. "And tell nobody. I don't want this getting out and the person who did this knows we're looking into him—"

"Or her," he said, interrupting me.

"Or her," I added. "Are you still coming to the event tonight?"

"Of course, I wouldn't miss it for the world," he grinned.

"Don't be late."

"I'll see you when I see you," he mumbled as he walked away.

I fetched Detective Campbell from the station, then headed to the middle of nowhere forest between Boise and Ketchum. I turned onto the dirt road and stopped. There were cars lining the narrow road, making it difficult to drive past, so we parked in the nearest spot and climbed out.

"What are we looking for?" I asked, trying to catch up to the detective. When Steve had first arrived, I didn't really like him or wanted to work with him; I couldn't understand why we needed a detective from out of state when they could've promoted internally. Then I remembered they wouldn't promote me because of what my father did, and the other officers weren't at that level yet, so hiring him made sense even though I didn't agree with it.

Then the more we worked together, and I got to know him, did I realize he was all right. He was hardworking, didn't fall in with the usual crowd, and treated everyone with respect. I felt bad for his wife, though; she had gone through enough and I sincerely hoped they too could have a child one day. I only had one child, and although I didn't want another one, I had a healthy child and Macey was a supportive wife.

"To be honest, Officer Graham," Detective Campbell said, "I don't know. We need to speak with Craig Williams and Carol again. They must remember the other ladies, especially because they attended often." He sounded determined and, for the sake of the case, I hoped he was right. "Do you know where Officer Crick is?"

"He said he'd be here," I said, surveying the parking area. "I don't see his car. What about Detective Marshall?"

"He isn't able to make it and they don't have anyone to spare so it's just us," Detective Campbell said. "It's not like we will be doing anything. We're just looking."

We continued the rest of the walk in silence and as we

reached the top of the hill, flames from the bonfire, loud music, laughter, and screams flooded my senses. There was too much going on. The cool air whipped around me. A fire flared to life on top of the entrance near the office we had seen Carol emerge from, as well as a fire pit near the entrance where many patrons were waiting to enter.

"Wow," I said, "look what they're wearing." I knew about the kink scene, but I didn't really know what or who they were all about, but this was something different. I had never seen so many people wearing black leather in one spot before.

"You can say that again," Detective Campbell said, staring at the ladies in front who barely wore anything warm. "I'm amazed they walked up the uneven hill in high heels."

I chuckled. "There's Craig," I said, and we waved at him at the same time.

Craig did a double take, and his face dropped. "What are you doing here?" he whispered, closing the gap and blocking our view of the people in the queue. "You can't be here." He glanced around. "You'll chase everyone away."

"We found more women, Craig," Detective Campbell said. "We want to look around, and I promise we won't do anything that will chase people away. This is your last event, and we would like to see if anything happens tonight or you and Carol see someone who may be in danger."

"Like what? And who are these women?" He glanced at the line of people near the entrance, then ushered us up the stairs to the office. "Can we rather talk upstairs? Carol can help you with the women. As you know, I manage the event, not the details." He wiped sweat off his forehead.

"Thanks," Detective Campbell said. "We appreciate your help."

"Carol," Craig said, opening the office door and entering. "We need your help, gurl."

"What's up Craig? Oh, hi," Carol said, her face dropping much like Craig's did upon seeing us. Her shoulders slumped, then she leaned back in her chair.

"Do you remember seeing these women?" Detective Campbell handed her a list of the women and their photos. "And did they ever meet with anyone you know? We have records that the women frequented your event, so it's possible the killer may be here tonight one last time. Please, we need to catch this killer before he hurts someone else."

Carol took the piece of paper and swiveled in her chair to face her laptop and started tapping on her keyboard. "I recognize this one," she said, pointing at Rebecca and then showed Craig.

"Yep, that's Rebecca," Craig said. "But none of the others." His brows knitted together.

"Yeah," Carol said. "Rich girl who likes to flaunt her body and money in everyone's faces." She rolled her eyes. "Something bad was bound to happen to her. I mean, I'm sorry she's gone, but she wasn't exactly careful."

"Mean girl," Craig added.

"So, she wasn't a nice person?" Detective Campbell said.

"No," Craig and Carol said together.

"She's one of those people who wants you to be jealous of what she's got, and she has a lot of everything," Craig said. "The last time she was here, her brother arrived. They fought, and he dragged her home using his two personal guards. It wasn't a great evening, and many people went home after that, and I added her to the banned list, but she never returned." Craig glanced at the people below. "Please don't make a scene. This is the last event for the season. I can't afford to close early because of police presence."

I made notes while I listened to them, and it was interesting, especially since the killer had murdered Rebecca first.

"If women are being targeted, they need to be informed. I would hate for your business to close," Detective Campbell said sternly. "But right now, their safety comes first. You can work with us or we close you down right now and arrest everybody."

"That will kill everything I've worked so hard for," Craig said.

"Catching a killer is more important, don't you think?" Detective Campbell said, glancing over the railing below.

Craig visibly relaxed and nodded. "I'm sorry, you're absolutely right. Please excuse my behavior. I'll do everything I can to help protect the women."

Detective Campbell smiled. "Can you tell us if you know anyone who knew these women?"

"Carol," Craig said, "wasn't Rebecca last with Dameon?

Carol's eyes widened. "Dameon? Seriously? I honestly don't know."

"Who is Dameon?" Detective Campbell asked.

"He's one of our professional caners," Craig said. "And if I remember correctly, Rebecca enjoyed being spanked with a cane."

Detective Campbell shifted uncomfortably beside me, which made me feel even more uncomfortable than I already was. Right now, anything B.D.S.M was out of my comfort zone. I could understand someone wanted to enjoy a light spanking or to be tickled with a feather, but there were others who wanted to bleed, to be suspended by hooks, or even hit in the face to be marked by their Dominant.

There was much psychology behind it all that I simply didn't understand, and I suspected Detective Campbell felt the same.

"He's here tonight," Carol said, opening a screen on her laptop revealing he had already arrived. "Booth three."

"I'll take you there," Craig said, leading the way.

We followed Craig through the sea of half-naked bodies on an evening where everybody should wear jackets, thick pants, and boots. The wind cut through my jacket, and I was grateful I wore my thick jersey underneath.

Heat warmed the right-hand side of my face. I glanced in that direction the moment a woman walked past, swallowing her fire stick, extinguishing the flames, and when she pulled the fire stick out of her mouth, it ignited. She wore a silver body suit with black knee-high boots, had tied her hair in two ponytails, one beneath the other in the middle of her head, and as she passed, she winked at me. Once she was out of sight and the heat from her fire was no more, I continued walking, but by then Craig and Detective Campbell were almost out of sight.

I ran to catch up, passing a wooden enclosure. I stopped in time to see a large man bend over a bench and a tall woman, wearing a head-to-toe rubber bondage suit, pulling a whip out from behind her back. She was about to strike when a giant of a man stepped in front of me, closing the door. He grunted something I couldn't make out, nor did I want to stop him.

I hurried along and was relieved when Detective Campbell came into view. He stood behind a low wooden fence where spectators stood gawking at something. I turned to look, and my jaw slackened.

Craig jerked his chin in the man's direction. "That's Dameon."

"He looks like a killer," Detective Campbell said.

Dameon was naked from the waist up, with tight low-cut jeans he left unfastened. A woman beside me gasped when she saw him and blushed. Dameon was one of those men who won the lucky gene jackpot and only needed to gym once a week, yet still looked that great.

Dameon winked at the woman beside me, and she fanned herself. Dameon chuckled, turned his cold blue eyes on me, and winked.

"Tonight's lucky participant has been asking me to do this for so long that I couldn't turn him down again," Dameon said, enthralling the audience. A man appeared from behind the black curtains wearing nothing but something that reminded me of a cage on his private part.

Detective Campbell glanced at me, arching eyebrows. I shrugged.

The man stood before Dameon, who tied him to a torture device. Once Dameon had secured his wrists and ankles, he opened the top part of the device and the man stuck his head through, and Dameon locked his head in place.

"Now for the cane," Dameon said, approaching a stack of canes, pulling one with a black handle. "This is my absolute favorite cane. I've used it multiple times on willing people and I'm yet to disappoint."

Dameon then canned the man four times on his buttocks, followed by two across his back near his shoulder blades. The man's body revealed six newly inflamed welts. He seemed to dangle from the torture device like it was the only thing keeping him from crumpling to the ground like a used rag.

Two women and a man unshackled the injured man and carried him to the back.

"We will care for his wounds and ensure he is comfortable while he recovers," Dameon said, walking around the area like a circus ringmaster. Sweat covered his shoulders and face, and his eyes were large. He looked intoxicated. "Should any of you want to go on my torture ride, please make a booking with Carol at reception, and pay upfront."

"How much does he charge?" Detective Campbell said.

"Three-hundred dollars," Craig said.

"Wow."

"He's the best," Craig added.

Dameon bowed low, the crowd cheered, and he disappeared behind the black curtain at the back.

Detective Campbell seemed agitated as he asked Craig to speak with Dameon, and I couldn't understand why until Detective Campbell pointed at his wrists and neck. The killer could have used a device like that on our victims.

Chapter Twenty-Two

A DEVICE TO REMEMBER

Detective Steve Campbell

I stood across from Dameon with Officer Graham beside me. He kept staring at the man on the bed, who was enjoying the special treatment he was receiving. The red welts on his body were no longer as swollen or inflamed, and was having a whispering conversation with a young lady who kept combing her fingers through his hair. He seemed blissful in his blanket cocoon.

"Llewellyn did such a good job," Dameon said, kissing the one girl's cheek. "I prefer caning women, for obvious reasons, so for me to cane a man today was special."

"Why did you?"

"Because Llewellyn here wouldn't stop messaging me." Dameon rolled his eyes while a sly grin split his face in two. "And because he asked nicely, I had to comply, but only if he wore a cock cage. The last thing I wanted was for him having a bigger hard-on than me." He held Llewellyn for a minute, all the while reassuring him that everything went fine and he'd be as good as new before leaving the event.

"Do you cane all the time?"

"There's at least one new person a week," he said, getting off the bed.

Caning a new person every week surprised me, and it made me wonder what the sensations felt like, yet, at the same time, I shuddered, remembering the good old days when my father gave us hidings with his belt. "Do they always pay the three-hundred dollars to be caned?"

"Sometimes," Dameon said, shrugging nonchalantly. "Other times I accept donations."

"What kind of donations?" Officer Graham asked.

"A new cane or perhaps a flogger, and sometimes a play date. It really depends on the person and how well we get along." Dameon reached for his clothing. "Okay, I'm done," Dameon said, pulling on a thin white t-shirt. "Don't worry about him. He's getting the best aftercare from my girls." He winked.

"Thanks, but that's not why we're here. Do you know any of these women?" I asked, handing him the photos.

"Yeah, that's TrixieXXX, AquaVulva, and Almighty-Sub," Dameon said, pointing at Rebecca, Brianna, and Darby respectively. "I don't recognize that one," he said, frowning, and pointed at Melissa.

I glanced at Officer Graham, who was making notes of the ladies' kink names.

"Did you have any play sessions with these ladies?"

"I've caned TrixieXXX, but none of the others, and I have had play sessions with all of them. If you know what I mean?" Dameon said, wiggling his eyebrows.

I felt sick to my stomach. "Can you remember when these sessions were?" I asked respectfully.

Dameon thought for a while and sipped water from a bottle. "I honestly can't remember." He reached for his jacket and pulled out his cell phone. "I may have added it in my calendar." He browsed on his phone, mumbling to himself.

Craig tapped the side of his leg and glanced around.

"You don't have to stay if you need to be somewhere else," I said to Craig. "I'm sure we can find our way out of here when we're done."

"Don't scare my patrons," Craig said, pointing at me. "But I have to go. There are events that need setting up."

"We promise not to cause chaos," I grinned.

"Okay," Dameon said, nodding. "TrixieXXX was the second of last month, AquaVulva was the second of the previous month, and AlmightySub was the month before, also on the second." He switched off his phone and pocketed it.

"Where did you meet them?"

"I met them all online, then here at one event for a meet and greet, and then they came to my home for some special one-on-one attention." That grin of his was back, and I wanted to smack it off his face. "I have a spare room in my house I've turned into my own personal dungeon."

I imagined Dameon went through a woman every single evening and used the same type of activity for each. "What website did you meet them on?"

"KinkMe dot com," he said.

"Is that a dating site?"

"Yes and no, it's like Facebook but for the kink community. One can't search for something specific and they don't give you a certain number of profiles every day to swipe left or right. It's just profile upon profile one can browse, and even different countries. It's pretty cool. I have a few online subs I train and then some I meet if they live close by."

"And you didn't see any of the ladies the last week or two?"

"Nope."

"During your conversations with the ladies, did anything strange come up?"

"Define strange?" he said, chuckling. "When it comes to kink, nothing is strange."

"Let me put it this way," I started, "Did any of them fear for their lives? Did they ask you to help them in any way? Do you know of any other play partners they may have had that went wrong?"

"TrixieXXX comes from this super wealthy background and asked that I never say a word about our encounter or to publish any of the videos or photos I had taken of our play session."

A knot formed in the pit of my stomach. "Did the women have your permission to record these sessions?" I asked as heat crept up my neck.

"Of course, I'm not a creep, man," he said, raising his hands. "We always, always, go through what we're about to do and I ask if they would like a copy of the session. There are bad Dominants out there, but I'm not one of them."

I exhaled slowly, and my shoulders dropped.

"And the ladies said nothing about being in trouble or anything like that," Dameon said, sounding wounded. "Even in our online conversations, they were all normal, you know." He shrugged nonchalantly. "Speaking of which, I have another session back home, so I've got to run."

"Before you go, can you give us your details so that we can contact you, and here's my card if you think of anything else."

We exited the small room that stood behind the area where Dameon had caned Llewellyn, and traversed through the sea of bodies swarming into the various kinky enclosures. The moon shone brightly, lighting our way, while a cool breeze blew between the trees. There were fire pits placed sporadically along the wide path, with food stalls selling various takeaways.

"What's over there?" Officer Graham said.

They had a black curtain tied between two trees, and a tall man wearing dark jeans and a white vest exited. I caught sight of what was happening behind him and had to know more.

Officer Graham followed closely behind me. "What are they doing?" he said.

When a meaty hand rested on my chest, pushing me away, I pulled out my badge and asked him politely to step aside. The tall bouncer nodded and allowed us entrance.

A crowd of people filled the space. Some leaned against trees while others sat on the rocks Mother Nature had left behind. In the distance, they had suspended a man in the air with sharp hooks. I'd expected to see him in pain, but he smiled lazily and waved at everyone.

"I don't understand it," Officer Graham said beside me, gawking at the man. "That looks like so much pain."

"I know," I said, zipping my jacket up. Another breeze blew through the crowd, making everyone huddle into themselves. "Let's walk around one last time. I don't know what we're looking for, but let's keep moving. I'm freezing my nuts off standing here."

"Sure," Officer Graham said, turning to follow me.

As we approached the exit where the large bouncer stood, Officer Crick neared, his cheeks red.

"Where have you been?" I asked.

"Flat tyre," Officer Crick said, rubbing his nose. His eyes darted from us to the man behind us. "That looks awful, anyway. Have you found anything interesting yet?" He sniffed.

"We interviewed a man who had a play session with three of the women," I said. "And now we're just walking around before heading home."

"Okay," Officer Crick said, scratching behind his neck and then his forearm.

"What's up with you?" Officer Graham said. "You're more fidgety than usual."

"Nothing," Officer Crick said, glancing away. "Just tired." He walked ahead of us and stopped at one of the food stalls to buy a taco.

"Has he ever behaved like that before?" I asked.

Officer Graham shook his head. "No, but then again, I never interact with him outside of work."

"Okay," I said, still staring at Officer Crick, who fidgeted more than I'd ever seen him fidget before. I needed to change the subject. "I know I told you to hold off with that other investigation, but what was the last thing you did there?" We passed Officer Crick as he paid for his taco, then I glanced at another session where they tied a naked woman to a tree and whipped her back.

"I found footage the night the evidence went missing, but can't tell who the person is," he said, also staring at the naked woman being whipped. "They're wearing black and covered their face. And there's no other footage. I'm afraid we'll never know who stole Jack Haskins' parent's evidence."

"And there's no online trail of Jack transferring cash to another bank account?"

"No, but there is one transaction where he withdrew a large sum of money, so my best guess he paid cash."

"So, there's nothing?"

"Yep," Officer Graham said, staring at a man wearing leather hooves-like-shoes, a tail that was attached somewhere between his buttocks, and a leather thong. The man galloped across the path with a woman holding onto his reins. "And to think I thought I'd seen it all." He chuckled.

"Tell me about it." I grinned.

Officer Crick caught up to us, licking his fingers. "That was the best taco I've ever eaten. You guys want some?" he asked, holding out a second taco for us to see.

I rolled my eyes, pushing Officer Crick's hand away from my face. I stood staring at the people walking around; some went into the various events on offer, while others watched. This case was becoming harder to solve and time was running out. Something told me there would be another victim.

Chapter Twenty-Three

CONQUIN

Detective Steve Campbell

Detective Marshall handed over the scroll. The bodyguard opened it, read the two names printed and asked for our identities. We produced our identities, and he nodded, handing back the scroll, and opened the large wooden front door.

"How did you get us invitations so quickly?" I asked, pocketing my I.D. I stepped into the entrance hall and stared at the opulent room; enormous staircases, golden framed mirrors on all the walls, and near the front door was a map of Conquin; it was a maze.

"Violet," Detective Marshall said, smiling, and pulling me away from the map. "She'll be here," he added, winking. "And she's discreet." He glanced at the ring on my finger, and I felt very vulnerable, like kinky vultures were about to swoop down, tear my clothing from my body, and jerk me off.

I corrected my backpack on my shoulder and squeezed

the strap. Alice knew I was here. There was no way I could lie to her, never mind cheat on her. Leaving her home alone was enough heartache for me, and coming here made me feel cheap and dirty. I hoped nothing bad happened, or anything good.

"Gentlemen," a woman said, bringing me out of my thoughts. She reached for our bags, placing tags with our name and room number around the straps and handing them to a porter. "We'll ensure your bags are in your rooms, and here are your access cards," she handed us each a black card with a gold strip across it, "please follow me," she said with a smile that brightened her face and green eyes. "The others are waiting for your arrival before they start." She wore a black see-through silk dress with no underwear; she might as well have worn nothing.

Detective Marshall grinned and walked beside her, asking her name and where she was from. She giggled, grabbed his arm, then glanced over her shoulder at me and winked. That feeling of being watched hit me like a truck and I glanced up. In the right-hand corner sat a large, round, glassy object, and in the top left sat another one. As we entered the large dining area, there were more cameras in each corner.

I swallowed hard when at least forty heads turned in our direction. Their mouths salivating upon realizing we were fresh meat. I blinked and their sharp teeth and drool was replaced with laughter and some sipping on their drinks.

"I'm glad you made it," a man said, approaching from the darkness, proffering a hand. Detective Marshall shook first and then me. I didn't know where he had come from, other than the dark corner, because I didn't see him enter the room at all.

"My name is John_Bondage," he said, grinning. "We

are about to serve dinner, followed by whatever comes to mind." His signature grin was back, or it was a smolder, I couldn't tell the difference, but it was creepy.

"Thank you for having us, and then hopefully having us again," Detective Marshall said, smirking as he took in the sights of the pretty women sitting at the table or those servers who stood naked, waiting for instructions. "The food looks delicious. I can't wait to stick my fingers in them and eat them out." All I could do was stare at Detective Marshall; he was a pervert.

"Please sit," John_Bondage said. He fixed his black tie and pulled on his jacket sleeves. His suit reeked of money, along with his short black hair and glowing tanned skin. He looked like he fell out of a men's bodybuilder magazine. I couldn't see much of his face because of the mask he wore covering his eyes, but I'd never forget his grin; it was like the Cheshire Cat.

I sat across from Detective Marshall who already had his hands all over the lady on his right. We sat near the head of the table with Violet—who had a mask over her eyes, and wore a black, satin nightdress that hugged her figure—sitting on my left, and a woman wearing a short golden nightdress that just covered the important parts; when she moved quickly, she flashed everything to me.

I suddenly felt hot and overdressed in my black suit, even though all the men wore suits, and most wore masks covering their eyes.

"Hi," the lady in the golden nightdress said, reaching for my hand, "I'm Wendy."

"Is that your real name?"

"Oh heavens no," she said, giggling, and removed her hand from mine. "I'm Wendy-Wanks-You," she added with a wink.

I almost spat the water I had just sipped but managed to keep my mouth closed and swallowed, coughing into my hand and wiping my mouth and arm with the material napkin.

Wendy-Wanks-You giggled again and spoke to the person on her other side.

I flinched when Violet grabbed my forearm. "You look nice," she purred near my ear. "Does your wife know you're here?"

I cleared my throat and nodded. "Yes, and you? Any partner to speak of?"

"No, I much prefer the company of someone new and exciting every other month. I don't normally attend these weekend events, but because of my dungeon, I'm considered VIP." She rolled her eyes. "Anyway, I know why you're here and if I had to guess whether someone here could do those things to the women, I'd put my money on either Sinful_Simon or Dark_Wolf." She nodded toward two men sitting at the end of the table.

"I'll keep an eye on them," I said, glancing in their direction.

It amazed me that such a large table existed, but even more so, the large room in which it sat. Everything about this place was big; large vases filled corners, portraits hung from walls, and in the center of this room hung a large glass chandelier. I could only imagine what each room looked like, considering there were between forty to fifty of us attending.

"How does this work?" I whispered.

Violet smiled kindly. "It depends on each person, really." She enjoyed a long sip of champagne. "Some like to watch, others like to play, or there are private areas."

"And where do we sleep?"

"Wherever you want," her smile morphed into a naughty grin, "but if you want to be on your own, your room is like that of a hotel room, and there are no cameras in those rooms." She stared deadpan at me.

John_Bondage instructed the naked women to serve us starters, which was an elaborate dish filled with medium rare, sliced steaks with a sauce drizzled around the three slices. The tiny morsel wasn't enough, and I hoped the main meal was more than this; I may not be very kinky, but I at least brought my appetite with me.

As a server placed the plate in front of Dark_Wolf, he grabbed her arm, making her flinch. He pulled her down to his level, whispered something in her ear, and made her blush. He brushed his knuckles across her pert nipple, then kissed her cheek. She nodded and hurried back to the kitchen. He said something to Sinful_Simon, who agreed, taking a bite of his starter.

Dark_Wolf was like his nickname; messy, wavy dark hair that needed a cut, thick bushy eyebrows, and dark brown colored eyes. Stubble lined his jaw, thick lips that hid perfect white teeth, and if one looked closely, you could see the dimple in his chin.

Sinful_Simon was the opposite; neat, short blond hair, bright blue eyes, and a wicked grin. From the looks of some women at the table, they would gladly drop their underwear to spend a night with him.

The sounds of the party were a cacophony of conversation, utensils hitting plates, and music in the background. The three-course meal was absolutely delicious and if it wasn't for the roaming eyes and salacious activities that were about to follow soon, I wished Alice was with me.

During the meal, I watched and listened as much as I could for anything that was out of the ordinary for these folks. I didn't know what exactly I was looking for, but if the killer was here, perhaps there was a telltale sign. Unfortunately, I didn't think Dark_Wolf or Sinful_Simon were dangerous, they just looked like two horny men who wanted to enjoy themselves, but I'd still watch them and everyone here.

We knew the women had attended Conquin the same weekend and if this was the connection, our killer may have been here then. Whether he was here tonight, I didn't know.

The simplest thing to do was to ask the owner of this establishment, but upon speaking with Detective Marshall, he suggested we attend as guests. He thought we might find more information from the guests than the manager or owner, but as I watched the evening unfold, I realized he only wanted to attend because he wanted to play. Unfortunately, I couldn't get up and leave now as it would look suspicious, and if the killer was here, he would know we were on to him.

Once dinner was over, John_Bondage tapped his fork on his champagne glass and stood up. "You can enjoy your after-dinner mints in any of the rooms, except the library. We're having that room cleaned after someone broke in and ransacked the place. In all the containers you'll find various toys and protection. And all I ask of you, be kind, and always get consent for every single activity." He raised his hand, pointing his finger at nobody in particular. "Please folks, no means no unless you have pre-arranged for it to mean yes. And above all else, enjoy yourselves." He raised his glass along with everyone else.

Chapter Twenty-Four

CONQUIN - THE LIBRARY

Detective Steve Campbell

I held my arm out for Violet to take. "Thank you for accompanying me," I said. Having her walk with me made me feel less like a pervert walking around alone and gawking at everyone. If I had her to keep me company I'd look less suspicious.

"Pleasure, Steve, but you really should think of a nickname."

We passed a couple having sex in the long marble hallway, oblivious to the fact that we were there. The girl was holding her ankles while her partner was behind her, his hands gripping her hips.

"What do you suggest?" I asked, glancing away from the couple.

"How about Gentleman_S," she said, smiling. "You're a gentleman and your name starts with an 'S'. You won't forget it."

I chuckled. "Sure, why not." Having a nickname in a

world I knew little about was the first step in a direction I hoped wasn't a mistake. I sighed internally and flinched when Violet pulled on my arm. "What's wrong?"

"The library," she whispered, tilting her head toward the door on the left.

"Ah, the mysterious library that's being cleaned." I reached for the door handle, glanced left and right, but there was nobody around, and pushed open the door.

Once inside, I closed the door gently behind us and stared at the room. "I don't understand," I said, confused. "I thought it was being cleaned." When I said 'cleaned', I used air quotes.

Violet walked across the room toward the wooden desk and leather chair. "There's nothing here except a large calendar from the nineties," she said, then checked the drawers on the right while I opened the drawers on the left. They were empty.

A breeze lifted the curtain, which brushed against my pant leg. I pushed the curtain to one side and my eyes found a dark spot on the frame. Crouching, I inspected the mark.

"What's that?" Violet asked, her face near mine.

I glanced up to respond when all I saw was her cleavage and immediately looked down again. "I'm not sure," I said, clearing my throat. After taking a picture of the mark, I pulled out an evidence collection kit.

"Are you allowed to do that?"

"Well, technically no, but I want to know what this is and what happened here before it gets cleaned. See if you can find more marks." What I was doing was wrong. No judge would allow us to search the place just because the victims were here one weekend. They died weeks apart and nothing connected them other than this place, Craig's events, and three of the women had a play session with

Dameon. The evidence was sparse, and I was getting desperate. If I could find something tying the women here, then I had just cause.

I swabbed the red stain, bagged it, and placed it back into the inside of my jacket pocket.

"Steve?" Violet said, but there was something in her voice that made me stand up. She was staring at me and pointing at the floor-to-ceiling bookcase.

I closed the gap to see what she was pointing at when a coolness I hadn't felt earlier seeped into my bones. The bookcase lined this wall and in the middle was a gap where the two bookcases joined. I crouched and took out my cell phone for more pictures. I glanced up at Violet, who had paled.

I removed another evidence collection kit from my other jacket pocket and tweezers. I tweezed the chunks of hair and the flesh attached to it into the sample bag and pocketed it when the door flew open.

I shifted uncomfortably in the hard wooden chair, staring at Gerben, the tall, blond security guard with pockmarks on his cheeks, and green-colored eyes. He held the samples I'd collected from the library in one hand while the other held his cell phone. He nodded and said something to the person on the other end, then ended the call.

"You police?" Gerben asked with a Dutch accent.

"That's correct." There was no way to talk my way out of this, because my badge was beside his meaty thigh on the desk.

"For those women's murders?"

"Also correct." I'd gone over the story with him at least

twice already, but it seemed he needed to hear it a third time.

"The owner of the house already had police over to look at the library, yet you're the only one who found this." He raised the two samples.

"Not very good police work, if you ask me."

"I'm not asking you," he said seriously, but I noticed one side of his mouth had twitched upward. I couldn't help but wonder if police were called and searched the room.

"Who is the owner?" I said. The circumstances of how they managed Conquin were suspicious.

Gerben pursed his lips.

"I'd hate to go to a judge for a court order. There might be publicity. Reporters will come here to see what's going on. Nobody will want to come here for fear you will violate their privacy. What will your owner say then?"

Gerben visibly sighed and rolled his eyes. "It's John_Bondage."

"What's his real name?" I eyed him narrowly. "Judge, court order, publicity," I said, dangling the threat in his face.

"John Hunter."

I frowned. "The same John Hunter," I started, waving a finger in the air, "who is running for some political party?"

"Yes," Gerben said, pressing a finger to his lips.

"Yes, okay, fine. I won't say a word. He's married, and she isn't here."

"They have an arrangement," Gerben said. "Her wealthy father supports his political career, she is the trophy wife and does what she wants, while John does his politics, and she allows him to manage this place. But only if he remains anonymous. You are the only one who knows who he is. If this gets out, we're both dead."

I shook my head. I knew little about the goings-on of

what really happened outside of my work. The best thing to do now was to stick with the other reason I was here. "What really happened in the library?" I jerked my chin at the samples I had collected that were now in his hands.

"There was an altercation."

I glanced at the sample that held pieces of someone's flesh and hair. "That looks like more than an altercation."

"Two women fight over one man," Gerben said, rolling his eyes. He tapped on his cell phone and a moment later, two women entered the small office. "See," he said, jerking his chin toward the blond woman, then he pointed at his forehead.

"Yeah, I see," I said.

The brunette raised her silver-claw-like nails, which caused the lacerations on the blond's head, and hissed.

"But why say the library isn't to be used?" I asked.

"Owner wishes to put in new carpets," he said, tilting his head to one side and raising his shoulder. "After those two fought and spilled blood, the owner wants to make it look new again." He waved the women away.

"Can I stay?"

Gerben nodded, handing back the samples. "Stay, look, ask questions, but discretely. Owner wants person found, too, but without scaring people away. Understand?"

I nodded. "Understood." I pulled on my jacket and pocketed the items. I doubted I would send them in for processing now that I had the full story. It would be a waste of resources.

Gerben stood a whole head taller than me and stared down with his metallic looking green eyes. "Be careful, Detective," he warned in an ominous tone. "Many people here don't like cops poking around. There are lots of brittle reputations."

"I understand," I said. "Those that frequent here, do you think anyone might cause serious harm to any of the ladies?"

Gerben's top lip curled over his teeth, and he squeezed his eyes closed. "I don't betray."

"No, not betray," I said, raising my hands in surrender. "Just maybe point me in the right direction. Is there someone who enjoys hurting some more than others? Has there been an almost accident where someone was seriously injured? You know, stuff like that. And it seems to happen with the same person."

"Maybe," he said, then headed for the door. "Walk with me."

I followed the big guy down the servants' hallway and through a secret doorway and into another room where large couches and chairs waited for cheeky company to sit on them and sip alcohol and smoke cigars. Gerben closed the secret door—which was a large painting of a man on a horse—behind me.

We entered another room filled with glass walls, providing me access to view the next room, which held a bed in the center with tousled black satin sheets.

"They can't see us," Gerben said, folding his meaty arms across his chest. He pointed in the far right corner. "Camera records everything. One Friday, I hear screams and come running. Girl sitting in middle of bed with bloody nose and swollen eye, and marks around her neck." He motioned to his neck as if strangling himself. "I rewind footage, see man hurting girl. I show owner, owner says it's fine. I don't kick him out." He shrugged. "I can't do much. It's owner's home. But I watch him."

"Is he here tonight?"

Gerben nodded, then pointed.

Detective Marshall entered the room with one of the naked servers. I stood straighter and my shoulders tensed. Detective Marshall's right hand gripped the back of her neck in a possessive manner while licking her cheek. The girl averted her eyes, held her hands in front of her chest, protecting herself. There was something about this that made me uncomfortable. The girl looked disinterested. Distressed even.

"Say you want this," Detective Marshall demanded.

The girl squeezed her eyes shut.

"Say it!" he yelled, letting go of her neck. "Or do you want to be punished?" He loosened his belt and pulled it out of his pants.

My hands balled into fists. A cold sweat covered my body as anger rose within me. "How can I get inside there?"

Gerben placed a calm hand on my chest. "Wait, record a bit longer, then we stop."

"But the girl—"

Gerben shushed me and pointed at the glass wall.

Detective Marshall licked the girl's other cheek. "You want me to show you a good time, darling?" His tone was ominous. Then he gritted his teeth. "Answer me!" He yelled. His bald head was sweaty and his blue-colored eyes hardened as he stared at the frightened girl.

The girl whimpered, pulling away from him. "I need to go," she said, pushing his hands off of her.

"Not yet," he yelled, reaching for her arm. "I'm not done with you."

Gerben stepped away from me, opening a glass door on the far left-hand side, and entered the room. "Get your hands off her!" Gerben yelled, then called the girl over. "Come, your true Master needs you." The girl hurried across the room and into Gerben's arms for a quick hug.

The moment she touched his body, tears flowed down her cheeks. Gerben then released the girl, and she hurried toward the door and entered the secret room near me. She flinched when she saw me and sobbed.

"It's ok," I said, taking my jacket off and covering her. "I won't hurt you."

"What do you think you're doing, Gerben? I'm allowed to be here."

"You can be here, but you can't treat them this way," Gerben said, turning to look at Detective Marshall. "And if you lay your dangerous hand on another girl like you just held her, I will break both of them. You understand?" Gerben's threat made me stand at attention and not wanting to mess him around, but the detective disappointed me. He knew better. We were working on a case where someone brutally tortured and murdered women, yet he's doing this to a woman.

I entered the room and passed Gerben, calling Detective Marshall back.

"Hey, Steve, I didn't know you were here," Detective Marshall said, glancing nervously around.

"It seems I need to investigate you, Detective. Where were you the night someone murdered the women?" I asked, readying myself for a fight or to protect myself from him.

Detective Marshall raised his hands. "It's not me, Steve, I promise. I didn't kill those women. And yes, I have anger issues," he said, gesturing in the general direction of the bed. "And I get carried away sometimes—"

"Sometimes?" I yelled. "It sounds like you do this all the time."

"I know what it looks like, and I'm seeking counseling."

"Perhaps you should stay away from women for a

while," I said in a low monotone and trying to remain calm. "They recorded your actions," I glanced up at the cameras, "and I will go to your superiors, so don't test me. I won't ask for a copy. This isn't blackmail, but I want you to do the right thing. Okay?"

Detective Marshall nodded. "You're right," he said, rubbing his bald head, then scratched his red beard. "Give me another chance. I will do better."

"I know you can. Don't do this for me, do this for yourself. You're only disappointing yourself and your family. Improve on yourself. And stop tempting yourself. Stay away from Violet and any of these women. Or at least until you can learn how to behave."

Chapter Twenty-Five

THOUGHT PROVOKED

Detective Steve Campbell

After our little chat, I had assured Detective Marshall his secret was safe with me and that I hoped we could continue working together on the case. He seemed relieved about that and promised to keep in touch. I walked him to his room, instructing him not to venture out until he departed in the morning. Then I strolled to my room, which was on the other side of the hallway.

The sounds of delightful laughter echoed in the hallway, along with moans of pleasure. I smiled, knowing I had survived the evening.

After they busted us in the library, they took Violet somewhere else while Gerben had escorted me to that tiny office for our chat. She had done nothing wrong, and I had hoped she was all right and had enjoyed the rest of her evening. As I reached for my room door handle, a delicate hand reached for mine and I caught myself smiling.

"I hope you had a good evening, Gentleman_S," Violet

said. Her voice was as delicate as lace as her words caressed my face.

My smile reached my eyes, and I turned around. "It could've been better..." Then the question about her evening dissolved from my tongue when I saw her face, my smile fading. "What happened to your eye? Your cheek?" Her left eye socket and cheek were purple, blue, and swollen. "Who did that?" I asked, my voice raised.

"It's okay," Violet said, keeping my hand in hers. "I asked for it." She raised her head so that I could see clearly.

"What?" I yelled.

Violet unlocked my door, opened it, and pushed me through. "Not so loud, Detective. I really did ask for it," she said, closing the door behind her. "I wanted this." She proudly pointed at her marks.

"Why on earth would you ask to be hit in the face like that? I mean, how many times were you hit, and with a fist?" I reached for the bruise to feel if the person responsible had broken her cheek bone, but she grabbed my hand, pulling me away from her face.

"Have you ever wanted to be with someone so badly you'd do anything to be theirs?"

I swallowed hard. I had always wanted to be with Alice, and I did everything I could for her to be mine. It took a year for her to notice me, but once she did, we became inseparable. I nodded slowly, not liking where her train of thought was heading.

"In this world," she said, swallowing. "In my world, to be marked by the Dominant you want—you're in love with, would do anything for—is one of the best things a submissive could do. It's a way of belonging to Him; knowing that you're His and He is yours. It's an expression of love."

"But you're not a submissive."

"For this Dominant, I am submissive. I am His submissive. I know it's confusing, and I take my role as a Dominatrix seriously, but for this man I am anything he needs me to be."

"Then why can't you be with him?" I asked, the anger within me subsiding; but only a little.

She pursed her lips. "It's complicated."

"If two people love each other, they can make it work."

She looked up at me with tears in her eyes.

"Is he married?"

She nodded. "And he's in a powerful position. A divorce is out of the question."

"Does she know her husband is here?"

"Yes, she knows about what he likes and does, and she knows about us. The only reason she agreed to it is because I'm a Dominatrix and would never stay his submissive, and part of their arrangement is never get attached."

"But he did?" I asked, my tone softer.

She nodded, averting her eyes. "We both did."

She was right. I knew nothing about the complex nature of B.D.S.M or when two people fell in love who shouldn't; what could they do to rectify the situation, or would they continue their days in misery? I rubbed my tired face. It was way past midnight and I wanted to leave early in the morning.

I moved a lock of curly dark hair out of her face, and she glanced up with tears welling in her eyes. The moment she blinked, the dams would break, and I knew she would bleed emotions.

"Have a seat and tell me what's going on," I said, helping her sit on the single chair while I sat on the two-seater couch. I thought the distance between us was best. Now that I was in my room, I noticed the mini fridge and bar area. "Would you like a drink?" I stood up again and opened the bottle of whiskey and poured myself a drink and added some ice blocks. She nodded, and I poured her one, too.

Once seated again, I sipped the honey liquid and sighed. Violet did the same and smiled.

"So explain that mark to me." I wanted to find this man and beat him to a pulp. Nobody smacked a woman around. Ever. That's how my father raised me and thought most men did too, but obviously I knew little.

"Being in a dynamic with someone is just that much greater than being married. When two people want the same thing, and they want it to work, a relationship within a dynamic where there is a Dominant and a submissive, they are bound to each other in such a way that a marriage doesn't even come close."

She enjoyed another sip and continued. "Now I know you're married, and you'll frown at what I'm about to say. These types of relationships are intense. You get to know each other in a short amount of time, and each time you interact, it gets more and more intense. There's open communication, sharing our fantasies, and each person gives more of themselves than they would in a normal relationship or marriage. Think of it this way, how long were you and your wife married before you got to know her? And I mean really got to know everything about her, sexually or otherwise?"

I pondered the question she asked and enjoyed a long sip, almost finishing my drink. "It took about five years if I'm honest. There were lots of ups and downs," I said, shaking my head, "and lots of silence when things weren't going well."

"Exactly. Silence. A breakdown in communication.

These types of dynamics—well, most times. Don't get me wrong, sometimes communication in B.D.S.M dynamics breakdown too—but usually these types of dynamics the couple communicate their wants, needs, and desires up front. They negotiate, they plan, they ask, and they share. And because both are eager to please each other, it's just that much more sincere and intense." She licked her lips. "That's how I see it."

"I understand your perspective. I've read half the book you suggested, but marking someone like that is a little bit out there for me. It looks like abuse."

"Being marked like this tells me I'm his. I belong to him and only him. That we have bonded in a way that's unimaginable to normal, vanilla people. That I am his property, and he owns me."

"Like a thing?"

"No, it's more than that." She was quiet for a while. "It's hard to explain, but it's a sense of belonging, a bond like no other. That he and I are on a journey together."

"But why your face?" I asked sincerely.

"Some have their breasts marked, others their buttocks or backs, while some extremists prefer their faces." She pointed at her bruised eye. "I guess I want people to see my face when they come into the dungeon and know that I'm spoken for. That nobody, that no other Dominant, can make me his unless it's something I want. And I understand the backlash from those seriously abused by the ones they love. I don't mean to hurt them or trigger a lynch mob, but no one has ever marked me like this before and to me, it's an honor. I guess I just wanted to feel what it felt like, to really belong to him and to know that he was the one who did this to me." She smiled sadly.

"Then why do you look so unhappy?"

"It's part of the sub-drop. You know during the play session I'm on such a high and then when it's all over, there's a severe drop in emotions. It can happen to both the Dominant and the submissive and my sub-drop happened sooner than usual but that's ok. I just need to stay warm, hydrate, eat something sweet, and talk to a friend." Her smile widened, brightening her otherwise tired face.

I finished the rest of my drink and placed the glass on the table beside me. "Just as long as you're okay with what happened to you and I don't have to arrest anyone. I still don't fully comprehend everything, but I am trying to understand."

"That's all a girl can ask for." She winked.

Chapter Twenty-Six

NO PLACE LIKE HOME

Detective Steve Campbell

I tiptoed into the sunroom to find Alice on the daybed, fast asleep. I gently sat beside her and leaned forward, planting a delicate kiss on her forehead. She stirred and opened her eyes, giving me a lazy smile. "Hey beautiful," I said, kissing her on the mouth. "How are you?"

"Better now that you're home," she said, sitting up. "How was it?" she asked mid-yawn.

I wished I could share everything with Alice, but I couldn't, not about the things I'd seen. As much as I wanted to tell her about the excitement of such a party, I didn't want to share the dark side that accompanied it. A darkness filled with anger, abuse, and predators. There was much I still needed to understand, but it was something I couldn't share with Alice. It would be too difficult for her to grasp.

"It was okay," I said instead. "I don't think the killer was there, or at least I didn't see anyone who may have been the killer."

"How would you know?" she asked, placing her smaller hand on my thigh.

"I could tell by those who were there. Anyway, I don't want to focus on the case right now. It's the weekend, and I'd prefer talking about you and us. How was your evening?"

"It was good. Last night I invited Olivia over for card games and snacks, and then she went home after ten." Olivia was our next-door neighbor. "And she's coming over for dinner and you can finally meet her." Olivia had been visiting Alice regularly since they introduced themselves last month.

"I can't wait," I said, standing up. "I'm going to have a shower, throw my clothes in the wash, and then perhaps do some gardening."

"I'll join you."

For the next three hours, we spent our time gardening. It felt good to be outside in the warm sun doing something constructive and with Alice; it was a type of bonding we both enjoyed. We laughed at each other's jokes and even flirted a little. Alice was having a good day, and it warmed my heart to see her smile more than cry. I wanted to hold onto this moment forever where it was just us and nobody or anything else interfered.

Then, as the sun started setting, the doorbell sounded. As much as I wanted it to just be us for the evening, Alice having a friend meant more and I would welcome her friend into our home for the evening.

"That's Olivia," Alice said, washing her hands beside me. I would've preferred to shower before eating, but washing hands would do.

"What's for dinner, or should I go out and get something quickly?" I asked, drying my hands.

"Already sorted," she said, beaming. "I made a casserole early this morning that I just have to heat." She left me in the kitchen to open the front door.

I entered the room to meet our guest and stopped dead, cocking my head to the side. She reminded me of someone, but I couldn't quite place her. She had nondescript features, reminding me of every average-looking brunette with brown-colored eyes.

Olivia hugged Alice. Then, when she looked up at me, her expression dropped. "Uh," she stammered. "I'm Olivia," she said, proffering a hand.

I grabbed her hand and shook lightly. "Hi, I'm Steve," I said. "Your face is familiar," I added, pinching my chin with my index finger and thumb. "Do you recognize me?" I knew she did based on her earlier change in demeanor.

"I may have seen you at Violet's shop," Olivia said, glimpsing at Alice, then at me.

My brain did a somersault trying to place her in Violet's shop, then I remembered the geeky-looking shop assistant who manned the shop while we watched the security videos.

"Oh yes, now I remember," I said, and an overwhelming sensation washed over me having Olivia in my home. It was someone who may or may not be related to the case I was working on. "How have you been?" I asked as politely as possible.

"I'm good," she said, smiling.

"Who is Violet and what shop is this?" Alice said. "You never mentioned you were a shop assistant, or is this the sex shop you were telling me about?"

My shoulders relaxed. I rarely avoided the truth when telling Alice what I had been up to, especially when working on a case. So to hear that Olivia had already mentioned the sex shop to Alice relieved me.

"Yes, the sex shop," Olivia said, smiling. "And our shop may be involved in the case your husband is working on."

"Oh, really?" Alice said, smiling, but not really. "Is that so?" she asked me.

"I only went there to ask questions," I said. "I don't think the owner or the shop is at fault, but it was an interesting interview."

We sat down for dinner and spoke about everything except the case, the sex shop, or anything related to sex. I suspected Alice didn't want to go down that route and neither did I. The case was still active and although I doubted Violet was involved; it was best to keep her and Olivia out of my personal life, but, if Alice was becoming friends with Olivia, this could become tricky.

"So Olivia," I said. "Are you originally from Ketchum?"

"No," she said, glancing at her leftover food. She ate little as she continued pushing leftovers around on her plate. "It's one of those cliche stories," she looked up at me, "I followed a boy here with the promises of marriage, children, and the perfect home. He came here two months before I could and when I arrived, he had another woman living with him already. My mom had warned me not to leave and to stay with her in Boston. She died shortly before I left. That's why I took so long to move. I had no money to get back to Boston, but there was nothing for me in Boston anyway, so I found work here."

"Oh dear," Alice said, reaching for Olivia's hand. "That's awful. Where is he now?"

"The last I heard, he and his new bride moved to Las Vegas with their two children," she said. Her tone was softer and filled with sadness.

"You'll find someone who will treat you better than he

did," Alice said, tsk'ing. "I can't believe some men," she added, looking at me.

"What did I do?" I asked, teasing.

Alice laughed. "Not you, silly."

"Then why did you look at me?"

"Because you need to help us women rid the earth of those awful men." She laughed.

"I'm trying darling, I'm trying," I said, reaching for her hand and kissed the top of it.

"I've never seen you drive," Alice started, "yet you work so far."

"I bumped into a guy at the grocery store who works in Boise, too, and he introduced me to Violet. It all happened so suddenly and I was so thankful my life was falling into place, you know, especially after the rocky start. Right now I'm grateful for everything in my life. And I'm happy I met you," she said, beaming at Alice. "You've been so kind and welcoming."

"You're so sweet," Alice said standing up. "And it's a pleasure having you around."

"Let me help you," Olivia said, collecting the empty plates.

"Thank you, honey. The food was delicious," I said.

"Would you like to stay for a cup of coffee before you go home?"

"No thank you, Alice," Olivia said. "I appreciate dinner, conversation, and finally meeting Steve, but I must go home. It's getting late and I'm up early tomorrow. I get a lift into Boise every day and I can't be late."

"Let me pack you something for lunch for tomorrow."

"You don't have to—" Olivia started, then Alice shushed her, grabbed her hand and pulled her into the kitchen and packed her some of the salad and a slice of cheesecake. "Thank you, Alice," Olivia said, beaming. "I appreciate it."

"Sleep well and we'll have you over soon," Alice said, holding the front door open for her.

"Bye Olivia," I said, standing behind Alice.

"Goodnight, I hope you find the man responsible for your case," she said, walking down the path. She hurried next door, where she climbed the stairs to her tiny room above the garage.

"Who are the owners of the house?" I asked.

"That will be a Mr. and Mrs. Livingston. They're hardly home, off traveling somewhere exotic, so Olivia stays there rent free for looking after the place for them. When they're about to return home, Olivia dusts and opens windows, and makes sure his car is in working order."

"That's not bad," I said, considering the cost of living in Ketchum was so high.

"She's very lucky." Alice closed the front door and turned around.

I had had enough of cases and murders and other people. Right now, all I wanted was my wife, in any way she wanted me. "Shower?" I asked, feeling hopeful. I held out my hand for her.

Alice smiled and grabbed my hand. "Absolutely," she said, then let go of my hand and ran up the stairs, flinging her shirt at me. She hadn't done that in such a long time. I stood holding her shirt in my hands with my mouth gaping wide open. I glanced up at her and she gave me that look; the look that said she was finally ready for me to touch her. I did as requested and chased after her, yanking off my shirt. Alice kicked off her pants when she reached our room, removed her underwear and darted into the shower. I undressed and stepped into the shower after her. I grabbed her ponytail and spun her around, bringing my face near hers.

"Is this okay?" I asked, waiting for her response.

"Uh-huh," she said, grinning, her eyes hooded. "I've missed you, Steve."

"I've missed you, too," I said, and bruised her lips with mine. Our kiss overflowed with passion, lust, and all those good things. It was our first shower together in a very long time, and we were there for over an hour.

Chapter Twenty-Seven

MARKED

Officer Graham

I filled my mug with the freshly percolated coffee and headed for my desk. My phone started ringing as I reached it, setting my mug down and almost burning my hand.

"Hello?" I said into the receiver.

"Officer Graham?" the person on the other end said.

"Yes," I said, grabbing a tissue to clean the spillage on my desk.

"It's Detective Blayne from Gunnison."

"Oh yes, hi Detective Blayne. How are you doing?"

"I'm good, thanks. Listen, I went through the evidence collected from our victims and there's something you should know." I waited anxiously for her to continue her story. *"Tell your coroner to use a UV light on the women's chests."*

That made no sense. "Excuse me, what do you mean by that?"

"I asked our coroner to check our victims again and their families had claimed all but one. He checked his report and her body and found

something he had missed the first time around. There are letters written with invisible ink on her chest that become visible with a UV light. Ask your coroner to do the same and then let me know what you find."

"Okay, thank you, Detective, I'll do that."

"And to let you know, we're going back to the crime scene again. We're widening the search to see if we maybe missed something."

"Were there any shrines?"

"We found twigs and a shell with blood, but it was that of an animal. We found no traces or usable D.N.A."

"Okay," I said, making notes. I had to tell Detective Campbell and then Rachel. "Anything else?"

"Not right now, but I'll get back to you if we find anything else."

"Thank you, Detective."

"Good luck," she said. Her tone sounded hollow, but I felt hopeful, even if it was only for a moment.

Chapter Twenty-Eight

MARKED HIS

The submissive

Joan stared at herself in the mirror and smiled. She fixed her new leather bondage corset so that it didn't pinch her tiny breasts; it was one of those half-leather-corsets that fit her abdomen, then stopped under her breast with a choker and straps connecting them. She felt like a sexy-biker-stripper-girl, but decent if there was such a thing.

Joan giggled with excitement at finally playing with her dominant. They had been speaking online for three months and today was the day they would finally meet.

"It's time Sweet_Kitty," Sir said, standing behind her like the domineering figure he was. He was naked from the waist up, with tight-fitting jeans he left unfastened.

"Yes, Sir," Joan said, smiling and averting her eyes. She quickly passed him and stood near the bed, waiting for his next command.

"Lift your arms," Sir said. His tone was deep and throaty, making all the hairs on her body stand at attention.

"Yes, Sir," she said, doing as she was told.

Sir reached for the soft leather cuff, seductively fastening her right wrist first, then the left. Then he fastened the cuffs around her ankles, spreading her legs wider.

"Are you ready?" he asked.

"Yes, Sir," she said, squeezing her eyes tight and her smile widening.

Sir grabbed the crop from the wall and returned, standing a short distance away from her, and started the process of spanking her bum. One after the other, the crop cracked the air upon impact of her flesh and each time Joan stood still, accepting the wonderful gift from her Master.

The sound the crop made against her flesh was louder than the actual impact. Her skin stung, then warmed, then he struck again and again, until finally she felt nothing but the heat from the caress of his leather instrument.

"Color?" he said near the shell of her left ear.

"Green, Sir," she whispered. From the impact of their play, her excitement about what was to happen next, and all of Joan's feel-good-hormones rushing through her system, sent her on a high.

"Brace yourself, little one," Sir said. "I'm taking you higher."

When Sir disappeared, Joan shivered. His retreat left her cold, but before she could protest, the warmth of his hand on the curve of her slender waist and an instrument between her legs that once pressed on, sent pleasurable sensations throughout her body.

"Please may I come, Sir? Oh, please? Please?" she begged, unsure how much longer she could endure his delightful torture.

"Not yet," he said, teasing her some more.

"Please, Sir," Joan said desperately. "I can't hold it any longer."

"You may come," he said, and Joan released the orgasm she had been holding.

"Good girl," he whispered.

The sensation of Sir's pleasurable assault on her body rocked Joan into a different universe. She hummed and moaned as the orgasm went on and on, almost torturous. Never in Joan's wildest thoughts would she think an orgasm could become painful, but the longer Sir pressed the wand against her, the pleasure turned into a pain that sent her into a world where there were no thoughts. Where there were no internal voices telling her what to do. A place where she felt safe, warm, and cozy.

The power exchange between Joan and Sir was something nobody could take away from her. It was a bond between them so great, nothing could compare. It was an exchange that coursed through her veins as she felt Sir remove the cuffs and turn her around. He carried her onto the bed, where they would deepen their exchange through intercourse. This had all been pre-consented. Sir knew what he was doing and wouldn't abuse his power over her, and even if he did, Joan wouldn't mind. Right now he could do anything to her and she wouldn't be able to stop him; she was in her safe space, a place where he led her to, and she would do anything he wanted.

Joan wanted to be consumed by Sir. She loved him. She wanted to be with him; in all ways; his submissive, his love, the mother to his children. His. She knew the moment they started speaking online that this was the man she wanted. This was the man she wanted to be marked by. She wanted to be his in all ways; his property, his ownership, his everything.

Some would tell her it was too soon to have these types of feelings, but not for Joan. She knew what she wanted in her life now, and who she wanted, and she wanted Sir.

Joan's marriage had ended in divorce two weeks ago. The entire process was painstakingly long, because her ex was making everything difficult for her. It was Sir's online conversation and words of encouragement that kept her going. She couldn't wait to see Sir, but even then, she had to wait. He was busy with work. And when he finally said he was available today, she dropped everything to be with him.

Joan's thoughts flitted into nothing as the orgasms and sensations blurred her reality. She knew she was on her back. Sir sat on top of her. He came into view, then she blacked out; sucking in air and Sir came into view again. She wanted to reach for him but her hands were somewhere heavy. Joan tried to lift her legs, but she felt a heavy weight on them.

Joan coughed, choking on a thickness that made her gasp. She widened her eyes to see through the blur and fog as Sir came into view, then blackened out once more. She couldn't understand if this was normal; was this the subspace all the submissive's online had spoken about? It felt weird to Joan; it was the safe space she was in earlier, but very different. Her chest ached. She needed to get up and get fresh air. But she needed Sir's help.

"Sir?" she managed to say as thick spit dripped down the sides of her mouth and into her ears. "What's going on?" she asked, feeling confused. She no longer felt the sub-high she had experienced before. Instead, a strange out-of-body sensation took over, catching her off guard. Her body ached as if blood was being drained, her head felt heavy yet light, her eyes stayed out of focus, while her body became heavy as lead.

"Dream sweet_kitty, you were a delight for me to play with. Enjoy your slumber. I'll see you in hell," Sir said, making Joan flinch and struggle. But it was too late. Sir already had his powerful hands around her delicate neck.

Chapter Twenty-Nine

THE MARKINGS

Detective Steve Campbell

I entered the station, walked down the hallway and into the open plan office where most of us sat. Officer Graham was on the phone. When I reached him, he ended the call.

"That was Detective Blayne from Gunnison," he said, smiling. "She says we need to ask Rachel to use a UV light on the victims."

"Why?" I asked.

"There's a message."

"A message?" I asked, following him back out of the station toward his car.

We drove the eighteen minutes from Ketchum police station to the Wood River Chapel mortuary, where we found Rachel and her assistants busy preparing a body for a funeral.

"Detective," Rachel said, approaching. "What's going on?"

"Detective Blayne from Gunnison Police," Officer

Graham started, "says you need to use a UV light on the victims."

"UV light?" Rachel said, pulling disposable gloves out of a box. "It's not a standard practice that I do, but let's see," she said, pushing open the door and walking down the corridor to the room we knew as the Fridge.

"Their chest area," Officer Graham added, pointing at his chest.

Rachel opened the four doors for each of the victims and her assistant handed her the UV light. She removed the sheet, revealing Brianna's chest. Rachel switched on the light and held it above Brianna's body, revealing the word "*MINE*".

The assistant gasped beside Rachel, who didn't bat an eyelash.

Rachel did the same for the other three victims and there too was the word *"MINE"*.

"They wrote the same word in the cave," I said. "It's quite possessive."

"It's a sign of ownership," Rachel said. "It happens in the B.D.S.M world to mark the submissive as the dominants property."

"It's like the killer is saying the women belonged to him and he could do whatever he wanted with them." I shook my head.

"Yeah," Rachel said, gloomily. "It's awful."

"Do we have the results from what he had used on the cave wall?" I said, changing the subject.

"Not yet," Rachel said. "I'll follow up with them today."

"Thanks Rachel."

The lines between Rachel's eyebrows deepened. "I had phoned their coroner, and he never mentioned this to me."

"Detective Blayne asked him to check again," Officer

Graham said, "and like you, he doesn't use the UV light as his standard practice either."

"Makes sense," Rachel said, zipping the victims up and pushing them back into the fridge. "I'll have it tested but we'll just find the ink he had used, which is common."

"What do you make of the pieces of flesh taken from each victim?" I asked, remembering the leaf-shapes carved out of their backs.

"Trophy maybe," Rachel said. "They're all the same size and more or less in the same spot on each victim. I don't know why, other than to keep."

That was another piece to this case that left me nauseated. This guy was one of the worst killers I'd ever known, yet we hadn't been able to find anything on him, leaving me increasingly frustrated. *Perhaps it's time we got the FBI involved.*

Emily entered, waving a piece of paper in her hand. "Doc," she said, approaching Rachel. She gave Officer Graham a side glance, but he wasn't paying her any attention. "The lab called," she said, handing Rachel the paper, "and asked you to get back to them."

"Thanks, Emily," Rachel said, taking the paper and reading it. "It seems we have some results." She smiled.

Rachel was speaking with someone from the lab and writing on a notepad. Officer Graham sat beside me in Rachel's bleak office. They had painted the office walls white about fifty years ago and were now stained yellow. The broken blinds behind Rachel remained open, and sunlight streamed inside the room, highlighting the dust particles dancing in the air. The metal table Rachel sat at had a dent in the front from someone kicking it, and the chair needed repair.

"I'll receive new furniture next week," Rachel said, bringing me out of my zone.

"Oh, I ah," I stumbled, sitting upright in the chair. I felt like a kid caught staring by the teacher.

"It was all part of my conditions to work here."

"That's excellent," I said. "What did they say?"

"Some results came back," she said, pushing her chair closer to the table, and started reading from her notepad. "The items found on the ground near the victims had no traces. The shrines came back with nothing and the shells had cow blood, which they think came from any fresh steak pack. And the words *"MINE"* on the cave wall were cow blood mixed with soil from the mountain. They're still processing the traces I found on the victims and the piece of cloth retrieved from the tree."

"It doesn't help us solve the case, but at least we have answers," I said, standing. "Thanks, Rachel."

"Pleasure." Rachel stood and headed for her door. "I'll call you when we get the rest back."

Chapter Thirty

CASE REVIEW

Detective Steve Campbell

Back at the office I went through the file to see if maybe we had missed something, anything that could help us move this case forward.

Officer Graham was fetching coffee for us and would join me in the office, and would bring his laptop with.

I'd just sat down and opened the file when Officer Graham entered with our coffees. "I just received the list of people part of the Crown trust fund."

"I'd forgotten about it," I said, silently cursing myself. This was the biggest case I'd ever worked on. There were four too many victims, and each had their own story and leads which we had to follow up on, which meant things were being forgotten. "We need more people to help us on the case," I added, reaching for my coffee. "Thanks."

"Pleasure," Officer Graham said, sitting across from me and placing his laptop on the table. I was old school. I went through case files page by page and made notes in a notebook, and would only use my laptop where necessary. There was something about holding the pages in my fingertips that made the case that much more real to me. "Should we involve the FBI?"

"I was thinking the same thing."

"Until then, Captain assigned Officer Crick to work full time with us."

"We must keep an eye on that one," I said. If Officer Crick had used narcotics that evening we went to The Pleasure Zone, we may need an intervention. No police officer should indulge in illegal drugs. I hoped, for his sake, that the white substance around his nose was powdered sugar.

"I'm not one for ratting out other officers, but I've written a detailed report about that evening. I just haven't sent it through yet."

"Okay, let's first see before you do anything with it." Officer Graham was right to do this, but I preferred handling situations such as these with the person involved. As much as it relieved me that Officer Graham trusted me by sharing this, I had to monitor him, too. What other reports had he completed that featured me or anyone else.

Officer Graham started tapping on his laptop keyboard, and I read the report from Rachel on our first victim, Melissa. I read each word in that report, then went onto the next victim; Rebecca, who Rachel thought was the real first victim. The hiker found Melissa easier because something had interrupted the killer, or perhaps he wanted the hiker to find her first and confuse us with the rest of the victims.

The ladies had frequented the same places. Three of them had play sessions with Dameon. "We need to ask Dameon for the recordings of the victims," I said, remembering another action item I had forgotten about.

"Damn," Officer Graham said, shaking his head. "I'd forgotten."

"We need to make a list of all the things that are outstanding. As I go through the case, I'll add to it."

"Okay, let me phone Dameon quickly." He exited the office and went to his desk to make the call.

Erik knew Melissa and had attended The Pleasure Zone with her. Now that we had three more victims, we needed to find out whether he knew them, too. I made a note.

And we were yet to discover who this Monsieur character was, but so far he had only played with Melissa at The Play Spot & Anonymous Dungeon. I needed to ask Violet if the other three women had attended her dungeon, too, and if so, who were they there with.

And we needed results from Rachel still. My to do list was growing, and I felt consumed by this case; it was growing larger, and it felt like it was running away from me.

"Dameon will give us a copies of his play sessions with the women," Officer Graham said, entering the office.

"I don't understand it," I said, feeling nauseous. "He has all these play sessions with these women and records it as mementos. I mean, don't these women feel used. What if he puts these videos on sex websites?"

"I can't answer your questions, Detective, because I feel the same. It's a different world."

"As long as it's consensual then I'm fine with it. And no young girl or boy stuff." The world was a dark place if naive people entered it with their eyes closed. There was revenge porn, bad porn, people only in it to make money porn. And now one had the B.D.S.M aspect of it and here, too, predators lurked and preyed on the unsuspecting newbie. There were so many dangers out there that sometimes I was glad we didn't have any children. I sounded awful for thinking that, I would never say it out loud, but on the other hand it was also a blessing. I put these people away. If one of them had to hurt my child I would kill them. And that alone frightened me.

"I just received word that Officer Crick is off sick." He rolled his eyes. "I hope I don't have to submit that report, Detective. I would hate to ruin someone's career."

My spine stiffened. "Easy there, officer," I said, with humor in my tone. "Leave Crick. Let's focus on what we can manage in the case. Here's the list I've put together so far. Is there anything I've left off?"

"I'll go through my notes, but it looks like you've added everything," he said, sighing when he sat down. "It's a lot of work, but we'll manage. Hopefully, there isn't another body."

I read the report we had written for each victim while Officer Graham researched the sixteen people who were part of the Crown Trust.

"I can't believe sixteen people receive an allowance of two-hundred and fifty thousand dollars a month to do with as they pleased," Officer Graham said, nonplussed.

I couldn't believe it either. "That's ridiculous. Who are they?"

"They are all Crown," he said. "And the men marrying into the family changed their surname to Crown, too. That way, they get a hundred thousand dollars for being the spouse."

"Christ," I said. "Well," I said, shrugging, "each to their own, I suppose. Would you give up your last name for cash?"

Officer Graham thought for a while, then answered, "Everyone has their price and yeah, I just might." He grinned.

I crumpled a spare piece of paper and threw it at him. "Traitor."

"Hey," he said, laughing, and threw it back at me. I smacked it away before it hit me in the face. "Wouldn't you?"

"Yeah, I probably would." And I laughed and laughed until my belly ached. Officer Graham laughed with me, making me laugh even harder. He had that laugh that included a snort, which made me howl with laughter again. It felt good to smile, to enjoy myself, even if it was for a moment. My joy quickly vanished when my eyes moved from Officer Graham's face to the photo of Rebecca's decomposed body, and it felt like someone poured a bucket of ice over my shoulders.

"Hey, you okay?" Officer Graham asked.

"Yeah," I said, jerking my chin at the photo.

"Oh, yeah, it's sobering." And he continued tapping away on his keyboard while I scooped up the photos and packed them neatly under the reports.

I picked up copies of the newspaper clippings of the Gunnison victims and my mouth dropped open. The one picture was of a woman and a man with his arm around her. I squinted. "Is this the photo you mentioned seeing Erik?" I asked, showing Officer Graham.

He took it out of my hand and brought it close to his face. "Yeah, this is the one. It's very grainy and old but it does look like him." He handed it back.

"Yeah, I'll add it to the list of things to do." After I added that to the list my mind wandered to the families I'd met; Brianna Woods's daughter, Jane, had said Monsieur had texted her mom. "And we need to subpoena Brianna Woods' phone records to get this Monsieur's phone number." The list was growing.

We were silent for a short while when an officer I hadn't spoken with yet entered, sweat dripping down his temples from running. "Detective Campbell, there's a new one."

And I didn't need to know what he was talking about. I bolted out of the office with Officer Graham in tow.

Chapter Thirty-One

ANOTHER BODY

Detective Steve Campbell

I drove to the crime scene while Officer Graham kept telling me to slow down. "She's already dead. Killing us won't help solve the case," he yelled when I took the corner too fast.

"Sorry," I said, applying the brakes slowly. I squeezed the steering wheel, calming myself. "I can't believe there's another one. Docs Gunnison only have the four, or am I mistaken?"

"Detective Blayne said they had four."

"Why do we have a fifth one, then? I don't understand it."

We were silent the rest of the way, and I drove the speed limit. When I turned up the dirt road and parked behind James' wagon, I glanced at Officer Graham. "Are you going to write a report about my driving?"

"No Detective Campbell, but please don't drive like that again," he said, opening the car door and slamming it closed.

Fine, I deserved that. I'd been driving recklessly and couldn't afford an accident, but this case got to me. It shouldn't, but it did. I ambled up the path to the start of the hiking trail, which was silly considering I had driven like I was an F1 racer. The closer I got to the path we had been walking these last two weeks, I suddenly didn't feel like seeing who our latest victim was.

I followed the hiking trail until I got to a new marker and turned right. It was in the general vicinity of where we had found the others, and I followed the yellow tape that started near one tree, forcing me to step over rocks and bushes. A copse of trees came up ahead and as I entered the copse, our lights were on and positioned around her, shining brightly on her body.

"Christ," I said, approaching James, who was crouching near her body, collecting samples. "What did he do to her?" I asked as my eyes bounced from her head, the bruises on her face, to the cuts and bruises on her breasts, hip bones, and thighs. That wasn't the worst of it, this time there was blood everywhere.

"This is the primary crime scene, unlike the others which he dumped. It seems he carried her while she was unconscious. Maybe, for her sake, I hope she was already dead," James raised a shoulder, "then had his way with her. I'm almost too afraid to see what we'll see during her autopsy." I knew he was thinking of the results from the sexual assault exam.

I shook my head. This guy was sick and twisted. "She seems younger," I said, my voice breaking slightly.

"Yeah, eighteen," James said, standing and handing me her I.D.

"Joan Phillips," I said, more to myself than anyone else.

I heard someone throwing up in the distance, and without asking, I knew it was Officer Graham.

"I hate this case," I said, placing the I.D. with the rest of the evidence James had collected.

"You and me both, Detective. I wish this asshole would reveal himself so we could all take aim and shoot at him. When we catch him and he's still alive, he deserves the gas chamber."

I agreed with James; the case was incredibly gruesome. "Who found the body?"

"Anonymous caller," James said. "It's probably the killer."

"Probably. I'll see if we can get the info," I said. When Officer Graham neared, wiping his face clean, I asked him to phone the station and get the info about the caller and see if we could locate the area the call came from. He agreed and hurried back to the car.

James chuckled. "He isn't cut out for crime scenes."

"No," I smiled, "but he is great at researching and investigating."

"Perhaps he needs to stay at the office?"

"Maybe," I said, walking around the crime scene. "Did you place all these markers?" I asked, pointing at all the numbered yellow markers.

"Yeah," James said, standing again. "Every place where it looks like shoe prints, handprints, or something, I left a marker."

"There are tons. More than all the others combined."

"I know. I think he's fucking with us."

I grumbled my irritation and traversed on the outside of the scene, yet close enough to see what each marker represented. The area was damp, therefore it was muddy. I loved the smell of the forest, especially after it had rained, but the smell of iron seeping into the atmosphere left me feeling queasy. There was a heel impression from a boot, what looked like a palm impression, something that was just a hole; possibly from him kneeling in the mud.

"None of this makes sense," I said as I circled back to where James stood.

"Exactly, he is messing with us, Detective. He left all these impressions for us to find and I'm telling you now, he probably used a mould or something. I doubt any of the impressions are his. I'll be wasting my time testing it all."

"It's like he's bored playing with these girls and he can do whatever he feels," I said. "We need to keep a police presence here in the forest in case he returns." I hoped he didn't return, because if he did, that meant there would be another body.

"Detective," Officer Graham yelled.

"Yeah," I said, turning around and heading in his direction; I hated yelling.

"The call was untraceable, but I received a message from Detective Blayne from Boise and she says her team, with the help of cadaver dogs, found two more victims."

I didn't like this. "That makes it six victims."

"Yep."

"That means we have one more before he disappears to the next forest."

"Exactly."

Silence fell between us as we took in the implications of what we had just said. We were running out of time. "We have to find him, officer, and now." The hairs on my neck stood on end as the chilling thoughts of finding the last victim took hold of me.

"Yes, Detective," Officer Graham said gravely. "It could be tonight, tomorrow night, or the next evening. I don't know how he's choosing his victims, where he takes them, or why. We just have the result of his torture." He glanced at Joan on the ground and gagged.

I visibly sighed. My eyes darting to poor Joan, too. I didn't want to know who the next one would be or what he'd do to her. Whoever the killer was, he was one of the worst.

"What's this, James?" Officer Graham asked, standing near a bush.

"What?" James asked, standing.

The lines between my eyes deepened, and I closed the gap to see.

"Come, look."

James grabbed his camera and an evidence bag. He crouched, and with a gloved hand, picked up something. "It looks like a corset of some sorts." James lifted the piece of clothing and opened it.

"It looks like a big belt," I said, still frowning. "I've never seen something like that before."

"A woman wears this like a corset," James said, holding it out. "Then her breasts hang over it, and it's fastened using these straps that's attached to a collar around her neck."

"Like a dog?" Officer Graham said, sounding disgusted.

"It's B.D.S.M, Officer Graham, a submissive wears a collar and some have a leash attached to it. Then their Dominant or Master leads them around."

"Why?" he asked.

"It's a sign of ownership," James continued, "the submissive or slave shows their status within the relationship or dynamic by being collared. It's like a married couple who wear wedding bands, but in B.D.S.M, it's how the Dom/sub couple bond over their connection and solidifies their relationship."

"Oh," I said, while Officer Graham stared vacantly at James. It was an interesting way he had explained it. It made sense. I hadn't gotten to that part in the book I was reading. I still didn't understand the appeal, but if I had to guess for some people, it was better than marriage. That this type of dynamic or relationship they were desperate to belong to someone, to have that person take care of them in all facets of life and in exchange, they were everything to their partner. That their Dominant took it upon himself to be his submissive's everything.

"Is it all about sex?" Officer Graham asked.

"Isn't everything about sex?" James asked, chuckling. "In a normal marriage, a man provides for his wife. Does he not?"

"Yes."

"And his wife makes food, and in most cases, she's available to her husband for sex."

"I guess so," Officer Graham said, glancing nervously at me.

"From what I gather about B.D.S.M is everything is slightly more formal than a marriage. Well, most times. I think things have changed because the young guys are coming into it full of testosterone and want to have sex with every submissive that moves. Or they find a young, naïve, girl and just abuse her. But I'm not talking about that. I'm talking about the old school way of doing things that most people are attracted to. For instance, at formal dinners, the Dominant wear suits and they dress their submissive the way they want her to look. There are low, medium, and high protocols, depending on what one wants out of the dynamic; along with the level of control. And if one compares that type of dynamic to a marriage, they're more or less the same. Only in a dynamic, each person agrees to the role they want because they negotiate upfront and their lines of communication are much better than in a marriage." He shrugged and continued working.

"It makes sense," Officer Graham said. "It's basically marriage for the more kinky person."

"Exactly," James said, heading back to Joan's body. "I hope there's a fingerprint on this garment," he said, placing the corset in an evidence bag.

"I hope so," I said, feeling hopeful. "Okay, so Gunnison police have discovered two more bodies," I said, coming back to our earlier conversation.

"Yeah."

I rubbed my face. "There isn't much we can do here and we need to wait for the autopsy and any results that are still outstanding."

"What should we do next?"

"We need to get the recordings from Dameon, ask Erik whether he knows the other four victims." I glanced at Joan again. "And then to Violet's shop and ask her about the other victims."

"Okay," Officer Graham said with more enthusiasm.

Chapter Thirty-Two

FOLLOWING LEADS

Detective Steve Campbell

Dameon's house in Ketchum was on a hill with magnificent views. We had called ahead of time and he agreed to wait for us before heading out.

I knocked on the door, and we waited a couple of minutes when Dameon opened. "Detective," he said, opening the door wider. "Please come in. Can I offer you some coffee?"

"That will be great, thanks."

Dameon had a double story home with fine furnishings that looked like it came out of a catalogue. Officer Graham sat on a high-back chair and I sat on a sofa. Dameon had portraits of himself and his French Bulldog, but there was no animal running around.

Dameon entered with a tray of mugs and placed them on the center table. "Help yourself," he said, sitting on the sofa across from me.

"When we met with you, you had mentioned having

play dates with three of the women," I said, taking a sip of the coffee. It had a powerful aroma, but very delicious with the cream, no sugar.

"Oh yes," he said, standing up and approaching the tv stand on my left-hand side. He opened one side, revealing stacks of tapes with words on the spine. He flicked through the tapes and removed four. "I went through the catalogue after we spoke and I did in fact have a session with that other girly." He handed me the tapes. "These are just copies."

"Thanks," I said, giving the takes to Officer Graham, who had a bag with him. "We have another victim—"

"Another?" Dameon said, shaking his head. "What's up with this guy? He's giving us Dominants a bad name."

I showed him a copy of Joan's I.D.

"She's too young for me," he said sadly. "It looks like she's fresh out of school." He shook his head. Then recognition flashed in his eyes. "Wait," he said, leaving the room. "I think I know where I saw that girl," he yelled down the corridor, and went upstairs.

I didn't understand why, but his abrupt change in demeanor the moment he saw the latest victim left me feeling concerned. I placed my mug on the coffee table and stood to see where he went. Officer Graham sensed something too and stood as well, standing behind me. I reached for my weapon and rounded the corner. Placing a foot on the first step when Dameon traversed down the stairs.

"Detective," Dameon said, stopping on a step. "What's up?" he said, raising his hands. "I only want to show you this," he said, waving a photo. "Does this look like your girl?" He carefully closed the distance, his eyes darting from my face to my weapon.

I returned the gun to its holster on my hip and reached

for the photo. "Sorry about that. I wasn't sure what you were doing."

"No worries," he said, smiling uncomfortably. "Can we finish our conversation in comfort instead of standing on the stairs?"

"Yeah," I said, backing up without taking my eyes off him.

"I had a party here on Sunday with a photo booth and they left that photo behind."

Once Dameon sat, I took a seat and looked at the photo. "Where have I seen this guy before?" Our victim was standing in front of a man who had his arms possessively around her shoulders. Her eyes were wide, her mouth slightly parted, and her hands gripped his wrists as if she was pulling him away from her neck.

"Llewellyn," Dameon said. "He's the man I caned at The Pleasure Zone."

Before going to Erik's house, we stopped at The Pleasure Zone and they were busy packing up. I flagged down Craig, whose demeanor shifted when he saw us.

"What now?" he said, making known how unhappy he was seeing us. He bit the one end of the toothpick before spitting it out.

"We need the details for the guy Dameon caned that evening," I said, showing him the picture. Dameon didn't know the man's details and suggested we see Carol. "He may be one of the last to see our latest victim alive."

Craig shrugged. "I'm not sure."

Carol approached and looked at the photo, too. "That's Joan, or rather known as Sweet_Kitty. She was so young."

"And the guy?" I asked, handing her the photo.

"That's Jason, um," Carol said, thinking. "I think it's Hughes."

"I thought his name was Llewellyn?"

"Well, on my list he's under Jason Hughes. I'm sure of it."

"Please can you check," I said.

"Fine," Carol said begrudgingly, and ran up the stairs. A few short moments she returned with her list. "See," she said, pointing. "He's under Jason Hughes, his email includes a Llewellyn, and I even have a contact number for you." She smiled for the first time.

"Thanks, Carol." I wrote the number in my notebook. "What's that handwritten part?" I asked, squinting at the illegible word.

"I think that says Monsior or something like it," Carol said, frowning.

"Monsieur, maybe?" I asked, feeling like someone had thrown a bucket of cold water over my shoulders.

"Yeah," Carol said, nodding, still staring at her list. "Now that you say it like that, it is Monsieur. I just wrote it down incorrectly." She tsk'ed and fixed the word.

We never asked them if they knew of a Monsieur when we first asked them about Melissa. I couldn't believe we didn't ask. We could've prevented this girl's death. I didn't need to be punished for my mistakes because I was usually hard on myself, but this mistake got another woman murdered.

"Thanks," I said, sounding angry, and headed back to the vehicle.

"We didn't ask about Monsieur when we asked about Melissa," Officer Graham said beside me.

"No," I said. "No, we didn't." As much as I wanted to

beat myself up because of this mistake, we had to keep moving forward and find this guy.

Once we climbed inside the car, I searched for Jason Hughes on the laptop and got his address. "We can't lose sight of what we need to do," I said. I opened my mouth to say something when I swallowed my words.

"What is it?" Officer Graham said.

"Jason Hughes lives in my area." I glanced wide eyed at him, put the car into gear and smashed the gas. There was something about this that set off alarm bells. We lived in that area and Jason was a potential suspect. But what made it worse, Alice was home alone.

Chapter Thirty-Three

TOO CLOSE TO HOME

Detective Steve Campbell

I drove to Jason's house as fast as I could without causing an accident. I parked half on his driveway, half on the grass, and bolted out of the car, jumped over the flower bed and onto the veranda, almost driving my shoulder through his front door, which was locked. All I achieved was hitting my head on the wooden door from impact and an aching shoulder. I had also twisted my injured knee from sprinting and jumping, sending pain up my spine.

Officer Graham went around the back and gained entry into the house. I heard him call out Jason's name and announcing who we were. When silence greeted him, he opened the front door. "There's nobody here," he said.

I entered the house and searched upstairs for Jason or anything that could tie him to the murders.

"I'm not finding anything down here," Officer Graham said.

"Same here," I called from upstairs. There were no toys, tools, or anything connecting him to the kink scene.

My cell phone vibrated in my pocket. Violet. "Hi," I said breathlessly. "I'm kinda in the middle of something—" I started, then she cut me off.

"Steve, Monsieur is here," she said quickly and hung up.

"We have to get to The Play Spot & Anonymous Dungeon!" I yelled, jumping two stairs at a time and landed hard. More pain shot up my foot and injured knee. "You drive," I said, handing Officer Graham my keys and limped out of the front door.

While Officer Graham drove, I phoned Detective Marshall, who was near Violet's shop. It would take us less than three hours before we could reach the shop and would miss Jason/Monsieur. We needed Detective Marshall to take Jason Hughes, aka Monsieur, to their station for an interview. And he promised to keep me updated.

Officer Graham got us to Boise safely, affording me the time to calm down and think about our next steps. We parked outside the Boise Police Station, and I limped inside, my knee aching terribly.

"You okay?" Detective Marshall said, reaching out to help me.

"Yeah, I'm fine," I said, waving him away. "What did he say?"

"Jason is the elusive Monsieur. He denies hurting any of the woman, even though he admits being play partners with the women," Detective Marshall said, reading from his notes. "He said interesting things about Rebecca's family."

"Her brother had used force to remove her from The Pleasure Zone."

"Yes, that's right," Detective Marshall said. "Apparently,

when they found out what she got up to, they put a stop to it."

"Can I speak with him?"

"Yeah," Detective Marshall said, and started walking down the hallway. "He's still in the interview room."

"Hi Jason," I said, entering the room and sitting across from him. The evening we were at The Pleasure Zone, I had watched Dameon cane him. I didn't get a good look at him, but I did now. He had brown hair shaved short on the sides and cut neatly on top. He had sharp facial features with penetrating blue-colored eyes and well built for a man in his late forties.

"Hi," he mumbled, not glancing my way.

"That evening Dameon caned you, your name was Llewellyn. Why use that nickname if you use Monsieur?" Jason was a confusing character and I needed to understand his actions.

Jason glanced up and nodded. "Women respond easier to Llewellyn and are more relaxed if they know you have a real name." When he said "real name" he used air quotes.

I suspected when anyone was sitting behind their laptop screen they could use any name. Anonymity was best; you could be anyone all the time and nobody would know the difference.

"Do you know any of these women?" I asked, placing pictures of all five victims on the table in front of him.

"I've already told the other detective everything," he grumbled.

"Well, I'm here now so tell me again."

Jason sighed as he glanced at each picture. He pushed one my way. "She wanted a picture with me, and I complied, but she's way too young for me," he said, tapping Joan's picture. "I've had play sessions with Melissa at The

Play Spot & Anonymous Dungeon. And then a play session with Darby at her home, an online dynamic with Brianna, and a session with Rebecca in my home. Rebecca didn't want to get caught by her brother."

"Are you a Dominant?" I asked. It was curious to me he allowed Dameon to cane him, yet he had play sessions with submissive women.

"I'm actually a switch," he said. "I can Dominate and I can be submissive to a Dominant when I'm in the mood for a caning or flogging. It depends on how I feel in the moment and how dominant the Dom is, if you know what I mean. Some men are only really Dominant when the submissive is extremely submissive. When the submissive has a strong personality, the Dominant must truly work hard to earn the title of being their Dom. Those types of women are usually in charge either in the workplace or at home and need a Dom to take care of them when the need arises."

"Do you know if the women knew each other?"

He looked up at me but remained silent.

"Help us find the killer, Jason."

"Why?"

"If you know something, tell us."

"You already think I did it."

"We needed to verify a few things so that we can exclude you."

He sighed. "I honestly don't know if they knew each other, and I never spoke to them about who I played with. It's nobody's business what they did or what I did."

I sighed frustratingly. "Do you have other residence besides the one in Ketchum?"

He glanced away, nodding.

"Where?" I asked, pushing a piece of paper and a pen in front of him. "Write it down."

Jason did as I asked and pushed the piece of paper back. I took it from him, pocketing my pen. "We'll need you to stay here while we check this out."

Detective Marshall used the key Jason had given him to open the front door. We entered the living room, then into the open-plan kitchen. There was one room and a guest bathroom, and upstairs had two bedrooms and a shared bathroom.

"There's a basement," Officer Graham yelled from downstairs.

I ran down the stairs as carefully as I could and got to the kitchen at the same time as Detective Marshall. Officer Graham stood by an open closet that was actually a door leading down to the basement.

"I'll go first," Detective Marshall said, pushing past Officer Graham. I shrugged when Officer Graham glanced my way with a raised eyebrow.

"You can go next," I said, smiling. I brought up the rear and stepped carefully on the thin wooden stairs. I had injured my right knee from an accident years ago and if I ran too fast or jumped on it skew, that's when I injured it again, like now.

The basement smelled like damp cement and stale water. There was a dripping sound in the corner to my right. I walked around the stairs that stopped in the middle of the basement, and noted the washing machine, a tumble dryer, and a sink which were lined against the wall, with shelves above them filled with detergents. Against the back were more shelves with tools and a workbench. And on the other side were metal lockers, each one filled with sex toys.

I opened the last locker and a fold-out table almost knocked me on the head, but I caught it in time and laid it out. It was soft on top, with shackles attached to each leg.

"I think it's safe to say this is his version of a dungeon," Detective Marshall said, holding the crop and whip. Then he placed them back on their hooks inside the locker.

"Can we get the team down here to see if he spilled blood?"

"Yeah," Detective Marshall said. "I'll call them now."

While he radioed in, I went upstairs. "What now?" I asked when Officer Graham joined me in the living area.

"We still need to watch the videos from Dameon and finish the searches on the Crown family. Officer Crick is back today and has said he'll be looking into them while we're here."

"Okay," I said, nodding, "that's good. We'll find something. We have to." I sounded determined, but the clock was ticking and I didn't know if we would catch the killer before we found another body.

Chapter Thirty-Four

TO DUNGEON OR NOT TO DUNGEON

Detective Steve Campbell

I didn't want us going back to Ketchum just yet. While they processed Jason Hughes' house, we stopped by Violet's shop to ask whether she knew the other victims.

I entered the shop first; and something smelled like coconut assaulted my olfactory senses. I glanced to my right and noticed someone had opened and left a tub of coconut oil on a shelf.

Olivia was behind the counter, adding price tags to sex toys. "Detective," she said, her eyes wide. "What can I do for you? The other detective was here earlier and arrested one of our clients."

"I know," I said, smiling to put her at ease. "I only want a word with Violet. Is she here?"

"She's just busy," she said, thumbing behind her. "You're welcome to wait or I can call you when she's done?" She pointed at the velvety-soft red chair in the center of the room.

"We'll wait. There's no rush."

Officer Graham shifted uncomfortably beside me as we waited for Violet to finish with a client in the dungeon, and Olivia, bless her soul, tried to keep us company. But Officer Graham didn't want to be in that shop and he made it known.

"I'll be right back," Olivia said, moving out from behind the counter. "I just need to fetch more price tags."

Once Olivia was in the backroom that stood off to one side, I elbowed Officer Graham. "Will you calm down?"

"Sorry, Detective, but this place makes me uncomfortable."

"I know, you're making it known. Maybe rather wait in the car."

"No," he said, shaking his arms out, "I need to grow as a person, so I need to stay."

"Fine, just wipe the disgust from your features and smile. Be pleasant, relax your shoulders, and wait patiently."

"I'm going to walk around."

"Okay," I watched Officer Graham move from shelf to shelf, his features no longer revealing his disgust for the sex shop, instead he seemed curious. Being curious was much better than being judgmental.

A door closed behind me and I spun around as Violet entered her shop, wiping her face with a towel. The bruise on her eye was no longer visible, and I suspected she had used makeup to conceal it. "Detective, how did it go with Monsieur?"

"We're still looking into him," I said, opening the folder on the counter. "While that happens, I'd like to find out if any of these women came here. We found records in their credit card statements they were here, but I need to know if you recognize them and who they were here with."

Violet nodded and smiled kindly. "Sure, Detective, let me check the book." Violet pulled her book out from the counter drawer and placed it on the glass. She took the photos of the women and read the nicknames we had for them. "Yeah," she said, nodding. "They were here." She browsed through her book. "Yes, Melissa and Darby were here every second month, and Rebecca and Darby were here every month. Melisa was here with Monsieur. Darby had a different partner each time she was here. Rebecca had different partners each month, too, and sometimes she had two partners at the same time. And Darby had three partners she alternated with."

That was a lot of partners for each woman, but I wasn't here to pass judgement. They were individuals and enjoyed sex and kink. These days it was tough on women. They constantly needed to maintain a certain reputation or face alienation from family and friends. If a man slept with a thousand women, we celebrated him. If a woman did the same thing, we branded her a whore, a slut, or a prostitute. We didn't paint men and women with the same brush, unfortunately.

"Do you know who their partners were?" I asked.

"I'll write their names down. I only have their nicknames, unfortunately. And since the women paid, I only have their credit card details."

It felt like a needle in a haystack as we got more leads, but how would we check who these men were. I could contact Carol again. Perhaps the men used the same nicknames there. I felt overwhelmed with the backwards and forwards.

Officer Graham stood beside me when Olivia entered the shop, looking a little pale. "Are you okay?" I asked.

"Yeah, I think I ate something and not feeling well,"

Olivia said, approaching and clutching her handbag to her chest. "Violet, is it okay if I went home?"

"Is your lift here to fetch you?"

"I, uh, um," she stammered. "I'll take a cab."

"Who normally gives you a lift?" I asked.

Olivia glanced nervously at Violet, at me, then back to Violet. "I didn't know who he was," she said. Her chin trembled slightly. "When I saw him here, I swear I never knew he was Monsieur."

"What do you mean?" I pressed.

"Jason has been giving me lifts to work," she said. A tear slipped out of her left eye, and she dusted it away with the back of her hand.

"He always wore a mask, Olivia," Violet said. "I think he didn't want you to recognize him. It's all right. You did nothing wrong. You didn't know."

"Thanks, Violet, but I still would like to go home. You know, I just feel…" Tears welled in her eyes.

"We can give you a lift if you like?" I offered, reaching for the folder with the photos. "We can drop you off before we meet someone." We still needed to see Erik.

"Thank you," she said, smiling. "I'd appreciate that."

"Will you be able to come in tomorrow?" Violet asked.

"I'll rent a vehicle," Olivia said, trying to smile convincingly but failed. "I'll be here."

Chapter Thirty-Five

THEIR NICKNAMES

Detective Steve Campbell

We drove back to Ketchum and dropped Olivia at home. I asked Officer Graham to wait until she was safely inside before driving off. Then we headed to Erik Cooper's house.

The silver-haired, petite woman answered the door. When Esmeralda saw it was us, she opened the door and asked that we followed her to the living area.

"Sir Cooper will be here soon," she said. "I bring coffee."

"Stay there!" Erik yelled at someone down the corridor. "I have guests." His footsteps neared. "Gentlemen," Erik said, proffering a hand. He shook sternly, squeezing my fingers a little too much. "What can I do for you today?"

"We have more victims and would like to know if you know them or of anyone who would want to hurt them?"

He sighed, taking the photos from me. "Yeah, I have had play sessions with them." He handed the photos back. "Oh, before I forget, the last time you guys were here, I searched the Gunnison murders and you won't believe it. I knew one of the women. We had one play session years ago and she asked for a photograph. I don't know why they used that one for the newspaper." He shrugged. "Unfortunately, I won't be able to tell you who hurt them." He sat down.

Erik was forthcoming with information, and admitted to knowing the woman from Gunnison and the women from Boise. He had alibis. I didn't know if he was a suspect or not, but something told me we needed to keep watch over him.

"Are there any whispers in the kink community about what's going on?"

"Of course there is. Nobody likes it. The women are afraid, none want to meet up for fear of being his next victim."

"What are they saying?"

He leaned back, placing his elbows on the armrests, and steepled his fingers. "It's speculation."

"What is it?" I asked.

"I belong to a gentlemen's chat room on KinkMe dot com, and some Dominants were saying there are three dominants who could be responsible. Submissive's have come forward stating these guys pushed the consent boundaries."

"What does that mean?"

"During the negotiations, the submissive's didn't consent to strangling. Yet these three Dom's strangled them to the point of blacking out, and when they regained consciousness, the Dom's were nowhere to be found. When two people play, there's always aftercare, and these women received none."

"Do you know who they are?"

He nodded. "I only have their nicknames."

If we could get their nicknames and then join this website, hopefully we could figure out who these men were. I could ask Violet if she knew them, and possibly ask Craig and Carol even though they were hesitant to assist us. Our case was getting bigger, with more victims and more suspects. We needed help, and the FBI had the required skills to find the killer.

"Their nicknames are Dark_Chambers, BiteMeNow, and YourSolution."

"Do you have anything else to add?"

Erik seemed hesitant.

"Anything can help us at this stage," I added, wanting him to open up so we could further our investigation.

"In those same circles, I believe they are untouchable."

"What do you mean by that?"

"That they're protected."

The lines between my eyes deepened. "Elaborate please."

"I'm rich," Erik said, raising his hands. "I have money, I have connections, I sometimes get away with not paying a parking fine. But I could never get away with murder, not like these guys. They know people who know people and no police, or even the FBI, can touch them."

I had nothing to say. A nausea brewed in the pit of my stomach as I thought about these untouchable men and what they thought they could get away with. I understood the hierarchy of man; the rich and powerful got away with a lot, but a serial killer. I hoped not.

Erik raised a shoulder. "Sorry to say, but it is what it is, I guess."

"I don't know if we can trust him," I said, climbing into the car.

Officer Graham started the engine. "Me neither. We need the outstanding results from the lab. Maybe there's something there that we've missed," he said, putting the car into gear and applying the gas. "Of the men we have interacted with, who is rich and powerful?"

"There's a handful."

"Exactly, there's Rebecca's brother, Erik, Dameon, and John Hunter."

I rubbed my face. There were too many suspects and so far, they all had alibis. "We need to see if Officer Crick has found anything on the Crown's."

We were silent for a while. Officer Graham drove at a leisurely pace, under the speed limit. We were nearing the police station when I thought of something.

"That weekend I went to Conquin. Violet had shared something with me."

"Oh," Officer Graham said.

"Yeah, that she loved someone who could never be with her. He had punched her in the face because she had wanted him to mark her."

"I can't believe it," he said.

"I know. Anyway, she had also said he was in a powerful position and couldn't divorce his wife." I reached for my cell phone and dialed her number, but it went to voicemail.

"We have many 'maybe's' to consider."

"Yeah," I said, feeling dejected. "Now, which one do we look at first?"

Back at the station, I tried Violet's cell again, but it went straight to voicemail. I dialed the shop, and it just rang and rang. I didn't have Olivia's cell, so I dialed Alice's number.

"Hey babe," I said, trying to sound happy.

"What's wrong? You sound strange," Alice said.

"It's fine, honey. Do you have Olivia's cell number?"

"Yes, is something wrong?"

"No, no, it should be fine. But I would like to have it."

She read the number out to me.

"Thanks, babe. What's for dinner tonight?"

"Are you sure everything is okay?"

"I'll let you know later," I said, not wanting to lie to her. I usually promised when things were okay, but I honestly didn't think they were okay now.

"Okay, well, I'm making roast chicken and vegetables."

"I'm looking forward to that," I said, meaning it. The way I felt right now, I would rather be home with my wife, but I knew that a life or two might be in harm's way. "Love you," I said.

"Love you, too."

I ended the call and dialed Olivia's cell number, but that too went straight to voicemail.

"Officer Graham," I said, running to his desk. "Can we send someone to Olivia's home?"

"Yeah, what's wrong?"

"I can't get hold of Violet or Olivia."

"Do you think—"

"Yes, I'm going to phone Detective Marshall to get to Violet's shop," I yelled, running to my office, dialing the detective's number. Also, straight to voicemail. "What is going on?" I moaned to myself.

Chapter Thirty-Six

A SUBMISSIVE & THE DOMINANT

Their Exchange

Messaging exchange:

<Greetings Beautiful Angel 🩶

Dark_Chambers 48m Dominant 6w
XOXO

little_bunny 32m sub 6w
Hello…
Are you enjoying being a Dom?

Dark_Chambers 48m Dominant 5w
Being a Dominant is more than just a command. It's about being the person a submissive responds to without the Dominant saying a word. It's a meaningful glance, a look

that tells her everything. Has anyone looked at you like that before?

little_bunny 32m sub 5w
No, it sounds wonderful. Most of the guys on here are only interested in one thing.

Dark_Chambers 48m Dominant 4w
The kink scene has changed over the years, unfortunately. There are few Gentleman Dominants around. I'm part of a dying breed.
Tell me little_bunny, have you felt the bite of a whip, the sting of a crop, or the caress of a feather?

little_bunny 32m sub 4w
Not yet, Dark_Chambers. I haven't found someone who hasn't made my skin crawl.

Dark_Chambers 48m Dominant 4w
Do I make your skin crawl, little one?

little_bunny 32m sub 4w
No ☺

Dark_Chambers 48m Dominant 4w
Good.
You have nice pictures. I like the one where we don't see much. I prefer it when a submissive leaves much to my imagination. It leaves me wanting her more.
Would you like me to train you? To show you some things about this world?

little_bunny 32m sub 3w
Where are you based? I can't travel far, nor can I afford any of the dungeons.

Dark_Chambers 48m Dominant 3w
I'm in Boise.
And don't worry about the cost, we can first meet at a cafe of your choosing, and if you feel comfortable with me, you can come to my place. After much negotiations about what you want and don't want, of course.

little_bunny 32m sub 2w
OK, I'm in Ketchum. When do we discuss what our wants are?
But first, are you married? I don't want to involve myself with a married man.

Dark_Chambers 48m Dominant 2w
I'm single, as my profile suggests. We can discuss our wants and needs on here. You have nothing on your profile about what you want. Maybe tell me some things that you are open to trying? And can you send me a picture? Your profile only shows your beautiful eyes.

little_bunny 32m sub 1w
Do you have any references I can speak with?
I've added some things to my profile now; what I'm curious about, what I'm interested in.
You have no pictures. Can you share one first?

Dark_Chambers 48m Dominant 1w
I'm part of the Gentleman's group; have a look. You can get references there.

I've added a picture on my profile… can you see it?

little_bunny 32m sub 6d
I saw no references??
I've added more pictures to my profile…

Dark_Chambers 48m Dominant 6d
Can we meet?

little_bunny 32m sub 5d
I need at least one reference. Please.??

Dark_Chambers 48m Dominant 5d
Here's TrixieXXX I've had many play sessions with her. She's one of a kind.

Dark_Chambers 48m Dominant 3d
Where are you little_bunny?

Dark_Chambers 48m Dominant 2d
Bunny? Want to cum and play?

little_bunny 32m sub 2d
TrixieXXX isn't responding.
Do you have others?

Dark_Chambers 48m Dominant 2d
AquaVulva; Sensual_Suzie; AlmightySub; and SpicyPepper

little_bunny 32m sub 2d
SpicyPepper says she's only speaking with you now. None of the others are responding.

Dark_Chambers 48m Dominant 1d
If you aren't interested in an experience you'll never forget, don't worry. I'll move on to the next one. My time is limited.

little_bunny 32m sub 1d
Wait, I want to meet. How about tomorrow?

Chapter Thirty-Seven

A SUBMISSIVE'S DEMISE

The Dominant

"Hello little bunny," the Dominant said, entering the dungeon. "So glad you joined me." He approached the wall on the far left-hand side, taking his favorite whip. "Boy, were you difficult to get here. First you didn't like the cafe I chose, then you were hesitant about coming here. I had to hit you over the head," he said, reaching for her tear-soaked cheek. "Shhh, you're in my care now." He leaned forward and licked her face. "I'll dry all your tears for you, but first, I need to make you bleed."

Chapter Thirty-Eight

DANGER IS OUT THERE

Detective Steve Campbell

"Detective!" Officer Crick yelled, jumping out of his chair and running toward my office. "I found something," he said, asking me to follow him, and ran back to his desk.

I ran after him, grabbed a chair that belonged to nobody, and sat beside him.

"Officer Graham asked me to look into the Crown's. I started with the grandfather, then worked my way down."

"Yes," I said, egging him on.

"One grandchild married a woman who had a reputation," he said, wiggling his eyebrows, "if you know what I mean."

"Okay, so what?"

"Anyway, their children are Rebecca and Reese."

"So what? Get to the point, Officer Crick."

"Someone strangled their mom to death during one of her play sessions. At first they thought it was the father, but he was in Europe on a business trip. They found Reese's fingerprints everywhere. There's a file for him, but it's sealed."

"Juvie record?"

"Yeah."

"He enjoyed his first taste of murder as a kid and has advanced as an adult," I said. "And now he's most likely the one who had his sister killed, and the others."

"And get this," Officer Crick continued, "Detective Marshall's father was the policeman who arrested him."

My skin ran cold.

"What?" Officer Graham approached. "Who arrested who?"

Officer Crick told Officer Graham what he had said to me.

"I still can't get hold of anyone," I said. I'd tried calling Olivia, Violet, and Detective Marshall with no luck. I hated to admit it, but with Detective Marshall's anger issues and now this piece of information, I couldn't rule him out.

"I'll get hold of Boise's captain," Officer Graham said.

"Thanks," I said, thinking. "We need to find Reese. Do we know where he might be right now?"

"I'll make some calls," Officer Crick said, picking up the receiver.

I felt lost. There were things we needed to do, people to interview, but we needed to first find out where everybody was, and with a killer on the loose—who may be Reese or even Detective Marshall—, we needed to find them now.

"Captain Davis did not sound happy and wants us to send him the information on Detective Marshall," Officer Graham said. "And he isn't at the station. Captain Davis will get his guys to look for him in Boise."

"Thanks," I said.

"That was the housekeeper at the Crown residence,"

Officer Crick said, turning toward me, "and she says Reese is playing golf."

"Did she say where?"

"Ketchum."

We arrived at the White Cloud Golf course in Sun Valley with backup. After fighting with the club manager, he told us Reese was on the course, pointing at the hole he should be on. We traversed the path there and found Reese with four men drinking beer.

"What's going on?" Reese said, chuckling. "You all look as serious as a heart attack."

"Can we speak privately?" I said, calling him over.

"No, whatever you have to say can be said in front of my friends." He glanced at his buddy's with a sly smile.

"We know about your juvie record, Reese."

That got his attention, and he handed his beer to the man on his right. "I'll be right back."

"What? A juvie record," the man said, holding his beer. "What did you do, Reese? Steal a Rolex?" And the other men joined in laughter.

We walked a safe distance away from his friends before he climbed into me. "What the hell, man?"

"I warned you, Reese," I said sternly. "Now tell me what happened and what your connection is to these women, including the murder of your sister." I raised the photos of the women, practically shoving them in his face.

"I told you I don't know, and I certainly didn't kill my sister," Reese said, folding his arms across his chest.

"What happened the evening you had your security drag your sister out of an event?"

"She was an embarrassment. But I didn't kill her, and why would I even look at those other women. They're disgusting," he growled.

"What did you do to your mom?"

"It was an accident. If you read the report, you would see that. I was a kid," Reese said, sounding hurt. "I didn't know what I was doing. It was something my mom asked me to do often. It was that or she would hang herself behind her bedroom door. The woman was bored and a sex addict. It says so in the report. It took me years of therapy just so I could stop blaming myself for what had happened." He shook his head. "Mom was ill and should never have asked her child to do that for her."

"Where is Violet and Olivia?" I asked.

"Who?" Reese shrugged. "I don't know who you're talking about."

This was frustrating me. The best thing for us to do was to hold him until I found the women.

"I need you to come down to the station, please."

"What? Wait, no, it's not me," Reese said, struggling to get away from Officer Graham, but Officer Crick was there to assist.

Before heading back to the station, I drove to Olivia's place to see if she was there. Alice's car was in the driveway; the house was quiet. I parked in Olivia's driveway and ascended the stairs to her one-bedroom apartment above the garage. I knocked. Nothing. I cupped the glass door to see, but there was no movement. She hadn't made her bed, and there were cups and rubbish strewn over the kitchen counter. I couldn't see any movement after calling her name.

I descended the stairs and traversed the path down the driveway, and headed for my front door. I didn't knock; I used my key and entered. The house was quiet. "Alice!" I yelled. "Alice, honey?" I entered the kitchen and there were dirty pots and plates in need of a wash. The kettle still steamed. She had filled her mug halfway with hot water and the milk was still out.

I removed my cell phone from my pocket and dialed Alice's number. Her phone rang inside the house, left unanswered. I didn't like this. "Alice," I yelled again, running through the house and went upstairs. Our bedroom door was closed. I opened it with force, my shoulder hitting the wood so hard, it loosened the door frame and the handle broke.

"What happened?" I asked, trying to make sense of what I saw. Alice on the floor, holding Olivia's bloody and bruised body.

"He hurt her, Steve," Alice said, choking on a sob. "A man hurt her."

"What man?" I asked, tapping on my cell phone to call for backup and an ambulance. Once I had made the calls, I approached Alice and crouched. "Let me see," I said, lifting Alice's hand off Olivia's neck and chest.

Olivia lay unconscious. Her chest barely moving. She had a sheet wrapped around her naked body with welts across her chest and defensive knife wounds on her arms. And around her neck was the thickest bruise I'd ever seen.

"Olivia?" I said, reaching for her hand to feel her pulse. "It's Detective Campbell. I've called for an ambulance. Can you open your eyes?"

Olivia's eyes flitted open. She looked straight ahead and opened her mouth. She tried to talk, but no sound came out. The bruise on her neck most likely the cause.

"How long have you been like this with her?" I asked Alice.

"Not long, about five minutes," she said. It couldn't have been Reese because I was busy questioning him at the golf course.

Sirens wailed in the distance.

I stood. "I'm going to wait for them outside," I said. "Everything will be okay, Olivia. Alice?" I said, waiting for her to look at me. "I'm proud of you, honey."

Alice smiled. "Can I go with her to the hospital?"

"Sure, it should be fine."

I hurried down the stairs, careful not to hurt my knee any more than it already ached, and opened the front door in time to see the paramedics climb out of the ambulance. I explained who I was and what may have happened to the patient upstairs. "Try not to disturb the sheet too much. There may be D.N.A evidence." They nodded and headed upstairs when Officer Graham arrived.

"What happened?" he asked. I explained everything, and he shook his head. "He has an alibi."

"I know."

"That means we still have a killer out there."

"Has Captain Davis gotten back to you?"

"No, not yet. Any word from Violet?"

"No," I said, searching for her cell number on my phone. I dialed. Her phone rang and rang, then she picked up. "Violet?" I said, but there was silence in the background. "Who is this?" I said, glancing at Officer Graham. "Where are you?" Silence. "Don't hurt her." I threatened. I hurried to my vehicle. "Where are you?" And the person hung up.

"I'm already busy," Officer Graham said, and started

speaking to someone on his radio, asking them to locate Violet's cell phone.

I waited. I needed to know where she was before rushing out.

"She's in Boise."

"Where?" I asked.

"That weekend place." He hurried to my car, climbing into the passenger seat.

Chapter Thirty-Nine

IT'S NOT WHAT YOU THINK

Detective Steve Campbell

I got hold of Captain Davis and he would send police units to Conquin. I parked the vehicle at the Sun Valley field and ran to the helicopter waiting for us. We rarely used it for things like this, but this was an emergency. If we drove, we would get to Conquin too late. The drive to Boise was almost three hours long. There was no way we could get there in time. And I refused to wait the three hours. Boise police would get there in time, but I had to be there when arresting this killer. It was an ego thing; I'd been working hard on this case and wanted to be there when it ended. There was no way I could allow Boise police to arrest the killer without me being present.

Officer Graham climbed inside the helicopter first and buckled in. I followed. Once I buckled, I put on the headphones and said hi to the pilot, who gave us a thumbs up and pressed buttons and pulled levers to get the helicopter off the ground.

My knee bounced, irritating Officer Graham, who kept glancing at me and then my knee. I smiled sheepishly and stopped. Then when he looked out of the window, my good knee bounced again.

The flight to Boise was quick. We arrived at the Conquin helicopter pad at the same time as Boise police cars parked, their blue and red lights splashing across the large white walls.

Gerben walked out onto the large courtyard to see what the commotion was and when he saw me, his usual pleasant-yet-stern demeanor shifted to one I had witnessed once before when he threatened Detective Marshall.

I hopped out of the helicopter, ducked, and ran toward him. Officer Graham was right behind me. The pilot waited for us to get out of the way when he started hovering above the ground, then transitioned in his forward flight back to Ketchum. Officer Crick was driving down to fetch us from the Boise police station.

"Gerben," I said, waving.

"What are you doing here, Steve?" Gerben said, raising his hands. One police officer pointed his weapon at Gerben and told him to freeze.

"Detective Campbell," a short, bald man said, approaching. "I'm Captain Davis," he added, proffering a hand.

"Nice to meet you, Captain Davis," I said, shaking his hand. "Thanks for supplying the backup."

"No problem," he said, scowling at Gerben. "We're here to get rid of all the rubbish in our town."

Gerben ignored the remark and arched an eyebrow in response.

"Have you gotten hold of Detective Marshall yet?"

"No," he said, heading inside. "Put your weapons down,

men. You," he said, pointing at Gerben, "where is the owner?"

"What's going on?" Gerben asked.

"Where is John?" I asked.

"He's inside somewhere."

"Is Violet here?"

Gerben glanced nervously around.

"Gerben?" I said, stopping dead and grabbing his arm. "What's going on here?"

A nervousness I hadn't noticed on Gerben before seemed to leak through his pores. He fidgeted with his suit and headed in the opposite direction Captain Davis wanted to go in.

"I didn't understand what's going on," Gerben said, pointing left. "When John arrived with Violet, I thought they had a play session. They have one at least once a month, but she seemed..." he left his words trailing. "Scared." He pointed right, and we entered a second smaller room and Gerben shifted the mirror to the left and stepped into another secret room like the other evening I was here. "They aren't here anymore," he said, pointing at a room with a bed in the middle. The bed hadn't been made. There were portraits of John on the walls, tall plants on either side of the door, and a mirror above the bed.

"Is this where they have their sessions?"

"Yes," Gerben said, still anxious. "When they arrived, they headed toward his private room and when I heard the commotion outside, I entered to tell him something was going on, but they were gone." He shrugged. "I don't hear them."

"Does John allow others to watch him in his private room?"

"He films it," Gerben said, tapping the one-way mirror glass.

"Where does he keep the videos?"

"In his safe."

"Do you have access to it?"

"No."

I glanced up at two cameras pointed at the bed. Everything about this house gave me the creeps. "Is there somewhere else they could've gone?"

"I don't know," Gerben said, thinking, then he shook his head. "Lately, John has been busy in the west wing. We don't use it, and he has forbidden me from going there."

"Perhaps it's time you do."

The part of this mansion I had seen that weekend paled to the west wing. We followed Gerben down a long, dark passage that made my skin crawl. There were officers positioned outside the mansion and all over the vast land, in case John slipped past everyone.

Gerben opened the door onto a ballroom with black and white squared tiled flooring. There were large golden framed mirrors on the walls with a large glass chandelier dangling in the center of the ceiling.

The next room made me think twice about entering. The walls were a deep red color, with various medieval tools hanging on the walls, and scattered across the floor were torture devices that would maim or kill; there was nothing kinky or pleasurable about this room.

"What the...?" Captain Davis said, stopping in the center of the room between a Judas Cradle and The Rack. He reached for something on the cradle, wiping it with his gloved finger. "I'd give my left testicle this is human blood. He tortured the women here."

My eyes danced across the devices with plaques naming them; an Iron Chair, Breast Ripper, Brazen Bull, Dunking Stool, Pillory, The Iron Maiden, Pear of Anguish, Spanish Donkey, and The Scavenger's Daughter.

My mind thought back to the victims and what their bodies looked like, and how he viciously raped them. This was definitely the place.

"Detective," a man's voice boomed from the surrounding speakers. "So glad you could join us. You want Violet?" he said in a taunting voice, making my arms pebble.

"Where is she?" I yelled. "And show yourself." *Chicken shit,* I thought to myself.

"Come and find me," he said in a menacing tone.

"Gerben?" I said. "Where is he?"

"But, Detective, that's not John's voice," Gerben said, his eyebrows meeting in the middle.

"What do you mean? If that's not John, where is he? And who else has access to his house?"

Recognition flashed in Gerben's eyes.

"What?"

"Come," Gerben said, heading back the way we had come, but instead of going all the way, he opened the door off to one side that looked like a cleaning closet.

This house was a maze of secret doors and torture chambers, and I hoped they tore it down once this was all over. I racked my brain about who the voice belonged to and I went through all the interviews we had conducted and I came up with none.

"Is John the Dominant Violet was having all the sessions with?" I asked Gerben. I needed confirmation.

"Yes, his wife is part of the Crown family."

I stood still and Officer Graham crashed into the back of me. "Sorry," I said, rubbing my head. "Did you know this?"

"No," Officer Graham said. "Officer Crick mentioned nothing of the sorts. Perhaps he missed something."

"That's the connection to Reese, but what bothers me is someone injured Olivia and dropped her at home. She went to Alice for help and her bruises are consistent with the other victims."

Officer Graham stared blankly at me.

"I know," I said, squeezing his shoulder. "I'm also confused."

"Then who is the killer?"

"I thought it was John, but now I'm leaning more toward Erik Cooper."

Gerben stopped walking and glanced over his shoulder, raising an arm, bringing his fingers to his lips. He opened his mouth to say something when a bullet pierced the air, knocking Gerben off his feet and into the wall. He crumpled to the floor, unmoving. Everybody crouched with weapons raised.

An officer commando crawled to the doorway from which the bullet had come from and fired. Bullets whizzed over his head, smashing into the wall behind him, carving large chunks out of the walls.

"What bullets is he using?"

"The illegal kind," Captain Davis said. "Go boys!" he commanded and his police officers stormed into the next room.

Over the next couple of minutes, chaos erupted in all directions. There was shouting, weapons being fired, blood spilling on the floor. Officer Graham and I entered after them, took cover, and fired at the man holding the machine gun. He ducked behind pillars, large vases, and entered the next room unscathed.

The Boise officers followed the madman with the machine gun, but he kept them back with his firepower. It was no match for the guns we used.

There had to be another way to get to him. I didn't follow the rest of the men who went after him, instead I went back into the hallway and carried on straight, hoping I was right. There was only one door up ahead. I slowly twisted the handle, and it opened out into a kitchen. A door on the other side opened. Shots went off. I leaned against the doorjamb. The man entered the kitchen, shooting at the officers trailing him. I aimed. My hand shook. My right knee shook. I inhaled and relaxed. My leg stilled. I took aim. His head came into my line of sight.

"Why Erik?" I asked.

Erik laughed maniacally and turned in such a way he could look at me and those entering the kitchen. He aimed his machine gun at the officers and pointed a handgun at me. "What do you expect, Detective? I already have everything, but I couldn't stop there. I wanted more, and I got more. Then when I saw I got away with it once, twice, six times, why not again and again. I mean, come on," he said, laughing. "Eventually, everyone tries to do that which he may not do. And if I ever got caught, I have friends in high places."

I squeezed the handle. I hated how he thought he could get away with murdering so many women just because he knew someone. Nobody could get him out of this kind of trouble.

"Why the torture?" I asked. "It's so unnecessary."

"Why not? I mean, did you see those beautiful devices?

Wouldn't you want to try it on somebody? See how long their body can last." He laughed again. "The inventors knew what they were doing. And although I didn't want information from the women, I got to play with them."

"You're sick, Erik."

He shrugged nonchalantly. He didn't care.

"Are you the rightful owner of Conquin?"

His grin told me that was a *'yes'*.

Officers entered the kitchen.

He turned, raising his weapon to fire.

I pulled the trigger.

The bullet struck his skull, sending the front part of his face into the wall. Erik turned to face me, his one eye seeing me. His mouth opened in a surprise *O*. He raised his weapon, but he didn't pull the trigger because Captain Davis and his men entered, ending him.

Chapter Forty

WHERE'S VIOLET?

Detective Steve Campbell

Conquin mansion lived up to its reputation as a monster of a home filled with hallways, secret doors, and torture. We searched every room, but Violet was nowhere to be found.

I stood by the front door feeling frustrated with the turn of events. No matter what I thought, I couldn't believe I'd missed it. That it was Erik, the real estate tycoon. A bored millionaire who performed vile things on women who trusted him. Why? Just because he could.

I turned around to exit when my eyes landed on the map of Conquin, and I froze. My finger trailed the lines of the map outlining the plans and hope surged up my spine, giving me the boost of energy I needed.

"Where are you going?" Officer Graham asked when I hobbled toward the dining area.

I entered the large room where we had dinner that evening and stopped when I reached the one large vase, and yanked the carpet out of my way, revealing a trapdoor. I opened the door and found a pair of teary eyes blinking up at me.

The paramedics placed Violet on a stretcher beside John, who had been unconscious from the head wound.

"What happened?"

"John left me a message to meet him here. When I arrived, Erik greeted me, which was strange because I've never seen him here before. Then he pulled something from behind his back, and all I saw was darkness," she said, raising her hand for me to see the wounds on her head. "Then when I awoke, John was already unconscious beside me," she said, choking on a sob. "I didn't know where I was or how to get out. It was cramped and dark and I couldn't get out," she cried.

"It's okay," I said, comforting her. "You're safe now."

I held her for a moment, then let go. There were questions that needed answers. "Did you know Erik was the true owner?" I asked Violet, as the paramedic tended to the stitches on her forehead.

"No, John always said he was the owner of the place, maybe he only managed it, and Erik was a silent owner. I never saw him here." She flinched when the paramedic finished the stitch. "I never imagined Erik could be the killer."

"Do you think John knew about Erik?"

"I doubt it," she said, glancing his way. "You'll have to ask him when he wakes."

I nodded and wished her well. The paramedic wheeled her toward the ambulance and placed her carefully inside. Captain Davis asked that an officer join her and John.

My cell phone buzzed. "Hello," I said.

"Detective Campbell?"

"Yes, who is this?"

"It's Olivia," she said, her voice croaky.

"How are you feeling?"

"I'm okay," she said, but I knew she was crying. "Ask Violet who has the nickname Dark_Chambers?"

It was one name Erik had mentioned. "Okay, why?"

"That's who I met with. He is the one who did this to me."

"Okay," I said, then ran after the ambulance, opening the back door before they drove off. "Hey Violet," I said, waiting for her to look at me, "do you know who Dark-_Chambers is?"

Violets eye's widened, and she glanced at John. My shoulders tensed. I dropped my cell phone and reached for my gun. John sat upright on the gurney, the tubes and IV moving with him, and he reached for the police officer's gun. The officer noticed in time and spun around.

"Freeze, John," I said, aiming my weapon.

John lunged for the police officer. I fired. The bullet struck his shoulder. The policemen behind me went ballistic, and they pulled their weapons on me. Everyone started shouting. Violet screamed. John fell on the gurney, nursing his wound. The officer handcuffed him to the gurney, and two more policemen entered the ambulance. Violet was quick to jump out, tearing the stitches on her shoulder open again.

"What the hell, John?" Violet yelled. "It was you, too?" She shook her head. "You're poison. I hope you rot in hell!" Then she turned to me. "I can't believe I loved him. I allowed him to mark me." She cried into her hands. "He filmed our play sessions," she said gravely. "I'm sure he would've filmed the torture of those women, too. And you'll find them in there." She pointed at the mansion.

Chapter Forty-One

WHAT HAPPENED TO DETECTIVE MARSHALL?

Detective Steve Campbell

Captain Davis gave us a lift to Boise Police Station to wait for Officer Crick to fetch us. He parked his vehicle in his designated spot in front, and we climbed out. Before we reached the front door, a car raced past, then screeched to a stop. Screaming and yelling pierced the quiet air as Detective Marshall tumbled out, almost landing knees first on the road, but he managed to stand up without stumbling, tucking his uniform in his pants.

Captain Davis approached Detective Marshall like a man on a mission.

"Sorry, Captain," Detective Marshall said, stepping away from him with his hands raised. "Things got out of hand, then one thing led to another."

"Where were you? We've been trying to get hold of you all day."

Detective Marshall closed the door and the woman behind the wheel drove off like a fire was chasing her. "I slept in, and then I had a late breakfast." He tucked in the rest of his shirt and fixed his weapon in its holder. "And my cell phone battery died." He shrugged.

"Why didn't you tell me about your father's case?"

"What case?" Detective Marshall said, frowning.

"That he arrested the Reese boy for killing his mother."

Detective Marshall stared wide eyed at Captain Davis. "I don't know what you're talking about, Captain." The lines between his eyes deepening.

"You really know nothing about Reese's juvenile record?"

"No, Captain, I know nothing. As you know, my father died years before I joined the force. How could I know?" He shrugged.

Captain Davis was silent for a moment as he stared into Detective Marshall's blue eyes. "Okay," he said, grabbing his upper arm. "We caught the killers—"

"Jeez, I can't believe I missed all the action," he said, glancing over Captain Davis' head at us. "Sorry, Captain. I should've been here today."

"We'll fill you in on what happened, but for the next week, you have desk duty." Captain Davis spun on his heel and headed for the door.

"I deserve that," Detective Marshall said, heading our way. "So, who was it?"

"You won't believe it," I said, smiling. "But let's first get a coffee."

Chapter Forty-Two

THE TAPES

Detective Steve Campbell

We found the tapes under the bed in a secret compartment in John's room. He had labeled them with the nickname of each victim, along with others. We were yet to determine whether they were alive or if they were only play sessions. So far, Violet was the only one with three tapes, including the evening he hit her in the face.

I could only stomach watching two videos, and we skipped through most of it. John and Erik used those torture devices on the women; some were aware of their surroundings, while others looked like rag dolls being dragged around. The way they handled the women's bodies, it seemed to me like they were testing to see how long the women would stay conscious before passing out. The women would come to, then they placed them on the device, strangled them until they passed out or died. It was savage.

We kept the tapes, or snuff films, in a secure locker only

a handful of us knew about so that they, too, didn't disappear. With Erik gone, John was the only one left and he could place the blame solely on Erik because we only saw their faces a few times. The person who tortured them always wore a hood, and there were no visible markings on his arms. It could've been one or both of them.

Olivia was a witness and would testify that John was the one who harmed her. He had dumped her at home so that he could use his helicopter back to Conquin in time to help Erik.

I switched off the tv and spun around in my chair. "I've seen enough for one day," I said, standing. I'd only heard of snuff films, but watching them was gruesome, and I suspected we would need counseling afterwards.

"There are many still to watch," Officer Graham said, his face pale.

"This is going to take a while. I think I can only stomach watching one a day. How about you?" I said. And we would most likely fast forward through most of it. We needed to confirm whether the other women on the tapes were alive or not.

"One a day is fine by me," Officer Graham said. "What I don't understand, Erik gave us three names that everyone was discussing in the chatrooms."

"Yeah, Dark_Chambers, BiteMeNow, and YourSolution," I said, reading my notes.

"John was Dark_Chambers, and Erik was BiteMeNow. Who does YourSolution belong to if it's even real?"

"I don't know," I said.

"It's like he wanted them to get caught by giving us their real nicknames."

"They were rich and bored and wanted to see how far they could get away with murder."

"I suppose so," he said, not sounding happy. "I still would like to know who the other one belongs to."

"Do you think there are three of them involved?"

"Why not?" he said, raising his shoulders.

"It's plausible. If John can tell us there's a third one, then we can go after him."

"I doubt he'll say anything."

"Yeah, you could be right. But it doesn't hurt asking," I said, picking up my cell phone the moment it started ringing. "Hello?" I said.

"Detective Campbell, this is Rachel."

"Hi Doc, what's up?"

"The skin you gave us tested positive for the five victims," she said. They sewed together the leaf shapes that were cut out of each victim, making a square. Nobody wanted to touch it when we found it with the tapes.

"Thanks. At least we know we found the right killer."

"The shrines, shells, and sticks all tested positive for cow blood."

"Okay," I said, nodding and writing everything down even though she would send us the results.

"The two earrings that didn't match, and the worn leather collar had no traces."

"At least we know," I said. Erik and John placed those items there to confuse us, and by sending us down a path that had nothing to do with them. Yet, they left the newspaper clippings which I assumed was them bragging about what they could do to women. It was their twisted way letting us know that they wanted us to catch them. A dare.

"The blood found in Jason's basement was his."

"Okay." At least we could rule out Jason, aka Monsieur.

"And we have results back for the cloth found in the forest."

"Okay," I said, glancing at Officer Graham. He had found the black cloth and bagged it for testing along with the drops of blood found on the rocks.

"It's from a cold case," she said, followed by tapping on her keyboard.

"We don't really have capacity for a cold case right now."

"I know," she said. "I thought I'd let you know, regardless."

"Thanks. Could you send me the details? I can't promise I can look at it today, hopefully soon." I didn't want to promise anything, but I would have a look when I could.

"No problem," Rachel said. "Bye."

"Bye," I said, ending the call.

"What cold case?" Officer Graham asked.

"You know the cloth you bagged and the blood on the rocks?" He nodded. "It's from a cold case."

He raised both eyebrows. "Cold case. That's interesting. Let me know. Maybe I can look with you."

"We can look at it later. We need to sort this out first. There could be missing women in these videos we don't know about."

"I know, you're right," he said. "I'm heading out," he glanced at his watch, "already six. The day just flew by."

The day had flown by, and he was right, it was time to leave this for now and go home. "Before you go, send me the video you had found where the police officer took Jack's parent's evidence."

"Yeah, sure," Officer Graham said, sitting down again and opening his laptop. "There, I sent it to you." He stood up again. "See you tomorrow."

"Bye Officer Graham," I said, closing the box the tapes

were in and locked them away. Then I opened the attachment with the video and watched it.

I watched the video at least ten times pausing and rewinding at the one spot where the person dressed in full black walked quickly toward the evidence shelves. There was something familiar about his gait; like his hip had been injured.

I leaned back in the chair watching it for the eleventh time when it dawned on me. I remembered watching Officer Graham run after Duke, the cadaver dog, and I glanced out of the office. Not believing it to be true but after watching this and how Officer Graham walked, I couldn't help but wonder if he was the one.

I didn't want to react prematurely on this and would take it upon myself to investigate further; or rather, investigate Officer Graham a little closer.

Chapter Forty-Three

THE 6TH AT CONQUIN

The Dominant

After dinner, a small group of women joined Dameon in a room equipped with canes, benches, and a cross. He entered the room, unbuttoning his shirt and removed the black eye mask in order to see the crowd easier. He closed the door behind him, locking it. "I don't want anyone else coming in here and disturbing us," he said, showing the ladies his winning smile.

He flexed his biceps as he threw his shirt over the back of a chair, and the sexy lady sitting there smiled nervously. "Who might you be?" he asked, reaching for her hand to kiss.

"AquaVulva," she said with a quiver in her voice. She cleared her throat and glanced away quickly.

Dameon had that effect on women. No matter where he went or what he did, they were nervous around him. Their nervousness fueled his desires, giving him the energy to do whatever it took to pleasure them, and he would certainly pleasure all of them; keeping a video of their session as a memento.

"Pleasure to finally meet you, AquaVulva," he said, remembering their online exchanges. He then turned to the next woman, who stood by the window with her hands clasped in front of her. She was biting her bottom lip. He reached for her lip with his thumb and pulled it gently out from under her teeth. "Only I can bite that lip," he whispered. "You must be AlmightySub?"

"Yes, Sir," she said with a shy giggle, and quickly held her hands behind her back so she could push out her breasts, allowing him to graze her right breast with his elbow. Dameon grinned with a mischievous twinkle in his eye.

He then approached the third woman, the one he would cane tonight. "TrixieXXX, remove your clothing and wait for me by the bench."

"Yes, Sir," she said, and started undressing as slowly as possible and keeping eye contact with him.

"Good. Nice and slow, with purpose and determination." Dameon broke eye contact with TrixieXXX and walked around the room again to greet the next submissive he had been speaking with all month. "Sensual Suzie," he said, grabbing a fistful of her hair and lightly tugging her head to the side so her mouth parted, giving him access to her if he so desired. He didn't, not yet. But soon he would have her. Soon he would have all of them.

"I'm ready, Sir," TrixieXXX said, standing with her back to everyone and wiggled her bum.

"Good, girl," he said, and walked to the last one. "Sweet_Kitty," he said, reaching for her hand and pulling her up to stand. She wore a silk nightie that hugged her figure. "The youngest of them all, and I'm sure the sweetest," he said low enough so only she heard.

Dameon left the youngest and approached the row of canes waiting for him against the far wall. He picked up the one he loved using on newbies. It made more noise than it actually hurt.

He approached TrixieXXX with purpose, making her glance at him with wide eyes. She sensed his dominance and although they had already spoken about what would happen tonight, his approach still scared her; just a little.

"Open your mouth," Dameon said, placing the cane sideways between her teeth, and asked her to bite down. "Don't let it fall," he warned.

He reached for her left hand and raised her arm closer to the leather cuff, securing her. Then he grabbed the right hand, fastening her wrists. Next was her right leg, forcing her to open her legs much wider than she had expected, and she shivered in anticipation. He bound her ankles to the legs of the cross, then as he stood up, traced his fingers on the inside her legs, then thighs, as he moved farther up the apex of her legs. But he didn't touch where he knew she desperately wanted him to touch. He never touched them when he caned. No, he reserved that for private play sessions.

Dameon reached for the cane, and TrixieXXX licked the moisture from her lips. "Leave it," he demanded. He enjoyed seeing the mess they made on their perfectly made up faces. He wanted to see mascara running down her cheeks, and he loved it when their lipstick had smeared across their perfect lips. The women came in as perfect as they could and they always left a quivering mess.

"Ready?" Dameon asked, touching her shoulder lightly while touching her bum with the cane. He rubbed the cane up and down her bum at least five times, waiting for her answer.

"Yes, Sir," she said, squeezing her eyes tight.

"What's your color?" he asked.

"Green, Sir."

"Good." He let go of her shoulder and stood back. "I'm going to start with one hard one, then ten medium taps. Is that still okay with you?"

"Yes, Sir."

"I will ask you for your color after each cane and be truthful. I don't want blood or tears. I only want happy juices flowing, the juice from between your legs," he said, staring at the other ladies, who watched eagerly.

"Yes, Sir," TrixieXXX said, and shivered. Dameon knew that shiver. It was a shiver that told him his submissive would most likely experience an internal tremor and spasm that if he were to touch her, would definitely lead to an orgasm. But he would not. He loved leaving them wanting more. Wanting him. And then, when he had them, they would do anything he desired. And he would do everything to them.

"Here it comes," Dameon said, hitting TrixieXXX so hard in the middle of her bum where she had the most padding, making his arm shake. TrixieXXX did her best not to flinch or make a sound, but she bit her lip in response and squeezed her eyes shut.

"Color," he asked.

"Orange, Sir."

"Good, here come the rest."

Dameon caned TrixieXXX ten more times, one after the other, and each time asked her the color and she stayed orange. TrixieXXX had eleven welts on her bum, some raised more than others, but they were all a juicy pink.

TrixieXXX's legs shook as she strained against her leather cuffs.

Dameon returned the cane and approached Trixie-XXX, placing his warm palms on her bum, soothing the ache. TrixieXXX melted into his body as she absorbed his kind gift of aftercare. He placed his left hand around her waist as he rubbed a lotion on the welts in a circular motion. The warmth from his large hand was a comfort to his submissive as she floated into her dark, pleasant, happy space.

When a submissive was in this kind of trance, a dominant could literally do anything to her. To play with anyone like this, the submissive needed to trust the dominant completely. One small misstep and the dominant could injure the submissive, abuse her, and definitely hurt her.

But Dameon and TrixieXXX had gone over everything in fine detail, and they would have an audience. The chances of Dameon even trying to hurt anyone now were not on the cards. He would have his chance. Not now. Soon. Maybe.

Dameon loosened the cuffs, setting TrixieXXX free. He picked her up and placed her on the sofa, wrapping her in a blanket. He offered her some water and something sweet to eat. Then he climbed in behind her to comfort her and to look at the women staring back at them.

"Aftercare is important, ladies. If any Dominant tells you otherwise, he is bad news. There are many predators out there. Be wise. Finding anyone on that site and meeting them is the same as online dating. Meet them in busy places, don't go directly to their homes, and listen to your intuition. Always listen to your internal voice. It could save your life one day."

The women nodded and agreed, but they hardly heard

what he had said. He saw it in their lustful gazes, their own version of subspace just from watching his interaction with TrixieXXX. It didn't matter. He would play with them all, and then his brothers would take the game further. He didn't like that part of it and didn't partake. He enjoyed his own sadistic pleasure with them, pushing them to limits they would never otherwise reach with any normal, *sane* Dominant.

With TrixieXXX's back against his front, he decided to play a little, so he slipped his hands under the blankets and felt the warm welts on her bum. Then his hand went lower and deeper. TrixieXXX moved slightly, giving him easier access to her, soft, warm and delicious spot. They did not agree to this. He didn't care, TrixieXXX was high on her subspace and would most likely not even remember this. As he finger fucked her pussy, and with no lube on his thumb, he pushed inside her ass, making her flinch.

"It's okay, shh," Dameon said, leaning his heavier body onto hers, ensuring she couldn't move, then pushing his thumb deeper. TrixieXXX's eyes shot open as she tried to turn around, her expression letting him know she didn't like this game. "Don't worry, let me be YourSolution to your every need."

Next in the Steve Campbell Psychological Suspense Thriller Series

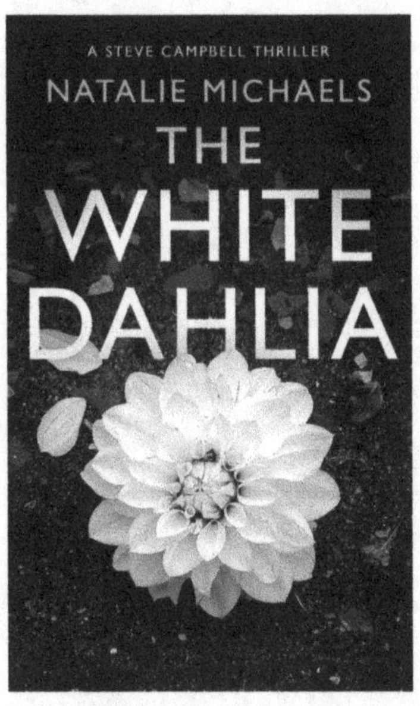

vinci-books.com/whitedahlia

A cold case reawakens. A copycat kills again. Can Campbell stop a murderer who knows history—and how to repeat it?

A brutal murder mirrors a cold case tied to the infamous Black Dahlia. As Detective Steve Campbell hunts a cunning killer, the clock ticks down. Can he uncover the truth before another victim vanishes—and the past repeats itself in blood?

Turn the page for a free preview…

The White Dahlia: Chapter One

THE SURGEON

The Surgeon reached for the sponge in the bucket, squeezed as much water out of it, and wiped her thigh clean. He dropped the sponge in the bucket, squeezed water out of it, and wiped down her shin and ankle. He wiped over a dark mark, smudging it over the top of her foot. The lines between his eyes creased. He continued rubbing until the mark disappeared. He rinsed the sponge, squeezed the water out, and wiped over that same spot until he was content nothing spoiled her porcelain flesh.

He soaked the sponge, squeezed it dry, and wiped. After he finished cleaning every part of her, he emptied the bucket and added fresh water for another round of cleaning.

When he was satisfied she was clean, her skin snow white, the Surgeon reached for the scalpel and slashed the corners of her mouth until her smile reached her ears.

Her smile pleased him.

Then, for the finishing touches, he cut chunks of flesh

from her thighs and breasts, placing them in a sterile tray for later.

He picked up the delicate flower and placed it carefully behind her ear, ensuring it stayed there.

The Surgeon stared at her in wonder; the way her hair framed her face, how her unseeing blue eyes met his, and at the shell her soul once inhabited. *Her.*

He smiled, appreciating his masterpiece, something he'd never replicate.

She was one of a kind.

A doll to admire.

His muse.

His Dahlia.

His.

The White Dahlia: Chapter Two

WINTER 2002: THE COLD CASE

Detective Steve Campbell

"Wait!" Alice yelled from the kitchen. "Your lunch," she said, running up to me with her hand raised, holding a brown bag.

I groaned inwardly. I still had a few pounds to lose, and Alice was adamant she would help me by making lunch daily instead of wasting money and buying delicious takeout burgers, pizzas, pastas, and anything with grease that clogged my arteries.

"Thanks, honey," I said, cupping her face and kissing her. She wrapped her arms around my waist, melting against my body, and dropped the lunch.

"Oh dear," she said, ending our kiss. "Your lunch."

"It's okay," I said, letting her go and crouching to pick it up. "What's in here?" I shook the heavy bag.

"An egg salad, and a sandwich with roast chicken and mayo on health bread." She smiled. "I know you get hungry, so I thought I'd make you two meals."

I beamed at her. She looked after me in all ways. “Thank you,” I said, kissing her forehead. “I’ll see you tonight.”

“Will you be working late?” she asked with sadness in her tone.

“I doubt it. It’s been two weeks since our last big case and things have settled down. From today, we’re looking into that cold case.” Yesterday we had finished reviewing all those recordings and it relieved me we could focus on something else.

Her smile returned, reaching her honey-colored eyes. “Dinner is at six.”

“I’ll be here,” I said, grabbing my keys.

The drive to the police station in Ketchum was quiet for a Monday morning. There were moms pushing prams toward the park, joggers running their circuit, and dogs on leads with owners smiling happily.

I parked in my allocated spot in the basement and headed for my office. There weren’t many detectives at Ketchum Police Station, therefore I was the only one with an office, apart from the captain, while the rest shared the open plan space next door.

Officer Graham entered my office with two coffees the moment I sat down. “Detective,” he said in greeting. “Ready for the cold case?”

As much as I wanted to complain that I’d just arrived and needed a few minutes to settle in, I didn’t want to kill his enthusiasm to solve cases. I smiled in response and placed my lunch on the ‘In tray’ beside my desk phone. “Absolutely,” I said, opening my desk drawer.

“Here,” Officer Graham said, handing me a folder and placing my coffee on the table.

The lines between my eyes deepened. "Is that it?" I asked, taking it from him.

"Yes, she's a Jane Doe, thought to be a runaway or a prostitute."

I opened the folder to a one-page statement and a detailed two-page autopsy report. The one-page statement provided bland facts about how they discovered her body and by whom. There were no follow-up interviews, no witness interviews, or pictures from all angles. There were four pictures; one from afar, the rest were closeups of her body parts. The way they had positioned our Jane Doe's body reminded me of something, but I couldn't quite place it.

"And this is from Dr. Brink." He handed me the results from the black cloth caught in a tree, and blood drops found on rocks. We had discovered the evidence together when investigating the murders at Sawtooth Forest near Bald Mountain.

"Thanks." I read the one-page statement written by a police officer who worked the Jane Doe case. "Have you called this police officer?"

"He retired the same year and died last year."

I glanced up at him, arching eyebrows. "Did anyone else work the case?"

He shook his head. "I called the previous coroner, Doc Lesley, who vaguely remembers the case. He said nobody claimed her body, nobody recognized her, and there was no evidence to process."

"So basically, he did nothing about her murder?"

"Yes."

"Were you here in 1997?" It was only five years ago, and Officer Graham had joined the force at least ten years earlier.

"I was, but I don't remember the case." He shrugged. "I've spoken to the captain about this case, and he is fuming because that officer didn't inform him about it at all. I don't think anybody knew about it except Doc Lesley."

That piqued my interest. "Do you think the police officer buried it on purpose?"

"Yes. It's the only logical explanation."

"This police station seems to have a reputation for removing evidence or hiding homicides." I was referring to the second case I had worked on since moving to Ketchum from Las Vegas, where the serial killer had paid off a police officer to move evidence involving his parent's death.

Officer Graham shifted uncomfortably, avoiding eye contact. "I'm waiting for the evidence to be sent to us so we can do a thorough investigation."

"Thanks," I said, standing, "but I don't feel like waiting. Let's fetch it now."

Officer Graham stood straighter and nodded, exiting my office after me.

The White Dahlia: Chapter Three

THE EVIDENCE

Detective Steve Campbell

I followed Officer Graham downstairs to the evidence storeroom. There was a pen and book tied to the desk where we had to sign in, along with the evidence we wanted. We were yet to upgrade our system, but for now everything was still old-school.

Officer Graham fished for the key as I was about to write in the book when Daphne, a junior officer, opened the gate from the other side.

"Is this what you're looking for?" she said, handing me the box.

I glanced at the label on the front, and it matched the case number in the file. "Yes, thanks Daphne."

"Pleasure Detective. There isn't much in there, but I'm sure you boys will solve it," she said. Her smile reaching her gray/green-colored eyes.

"We'll do the best we can," I said, tucking the box under

my arm. I was about to leave when I remembered. "Do we still have to fill in the book?"

"I'll do it for you," Daphne said, picking up the pen.

"Thanks," I said, noticing the ring on her finger. "Did you get engaged?"

Her smile reached her bright eyes. "Last night," she said, wiggling her fingers.

"Congratulations," Officer Graham said. "That was fast. Didn't you two only start dating a short while ago?"

"Yes," Daphne said, looking at me. "When you know you know, you know." She raised a shoulder.

"You aren't pregnant, are you?" Officer Graham asked. I shot him an annoyed look, but he was staring at Daphne.

"No," she grumbled, turning her back on him.

"Congrats, Daphne," I said, motioning for Officer Graham to leave. "Let us know when it is."

"Will do," she said, still busy with the book.

"What was that about?" I asked when we were out of earshot.

"Nothing," Officer Graham said in a huff.

"It didn't sound like nothing," I said, traversing up the stairs.

"The guy is a biker, Detective." He returned the annoyed look I'd given him earlier.

"Yeah, so?"

"Bikers are generally bad news. I'd hate for something bad to happen to her. She's too nice to marry someone like that."

I agreed with Officer Graham. Daphne was a lovely individual. She seemed gentle and highly sensitive, but we couldn't interfere in someone else's life. "Do you know the guy?"

"No, but—"

"But nothing, officer. It's Daphne's life and you aren't her ex-boyfriend or family. Until you have something concrete against this guy, leave it alone." I warned.

Officer Graham grumbled something I couldn't hear and walked off. I decided to leave it for now. We had a cold case to investigate.

I placed the box on our largest meeting room table and flicked off the lid. I stared at the contents. Inside was the victim's handbag that was found a short distance away from her body.

"Is that it?" Officer Graham asked, entering with the two coffees he had brought earlier. "I heated them." He handed me one. It relieved me his mood had improved. We had work to do.

"Yeah, this is it," I said. "Thanks for the coffee." I placed it beside the box. With a gloved hand, I opened the handbag and placed the contents out on the table; dark red lipstick, a business card for surgical devices, cash, loose tissues, and a fake flower clip. "Did they test these?"

Officer Graham placed the autopsy report and the one-page statement beside the purse. "No, there's nothing. They were just boxed and shelved."

"Call James and ask if he has time to process them now."

Officer Graham left the office to make the call. I picked up the warm coffee and sipped, wincing at the bitter taste. A shudder ran through me. I placed the stale coffee carefully inside the trashcan. I packed the items back inside the purse and placed them in the box, closing the lid. Removing the disposable gloves, I threw them in the trashcan and sat down.

The police officer who had investigated this case did a poor job. He failed to place each item inside individual bags to preserve any traces of DNA that may have still been on there. I doubted there would be anything for them to test after five years, but I still wanted it done.

"He's in the building and will be here shortly," Officer Graham said, entering the meeting room and sitting across from me.

It had been two weeks since I watched the video of a man resembling Officer Graham enter the evidence storeroom and remove evidence. I couldn't see his face, but I recognized his strange gait; like he had an injured leg and limped. I still needed to address this with him, but I first wanted to see how things went and if Officer Graham had other extra-curricular activities I needed to know about. Like that old saying, keep your enemies close.

"Morning," James McIntosh said, wearing the widest smile.

"Someone is having a good morning," I said, feeling some relief from my thoughts and matched his smile.

"Well," he said with a flick of his wrist. "Hubby has arranged a getaway weekend for us, and I simply can't wait."

"Where are you going?" Officer Graham asked, twisting in his chair to look up at him.

"Like I'm sharing that. The last thing I need now is for you and the missus interrupting our fun," he said with a wink. "I'll send you the details when I get to my computer."

"Thanks," Officer Graham said, and visibly relaxed. Sometimes one didn't know where James was going with his 'jokes'.

"I'm amazed Dr. Brink gave you time off," I said, leaning forward and placing my elbows on the table.

"I have so much leave due, and she didn't want me losing

any of it. Besides, you know what it's like. They don't like paying us for leave we don't use," he said, shrugging. "I have the Friday and the Monday off. I think taking long weekends away often is better than having a long holiday only once a year."

"I agree," I said. "Which reminds me, I need to do something for Alice's birthday." I made a reminder in my notebook. There was that new Italian restaurant I'd been meaning to take her to, and a weekend away would be most welcome. I needed it now more than ever, especially after the last case.

"Yeah, don't forget," James said. "She'll enjoy it. And we all need to rest," he turned toward Officer Graham and elbowed him, "even you."

"I'm taking some leave in two months' time," Officer Graham said, grinning. "And I can't wait to soak up the beach sun."

James stepped closer to the table. "Anyway, what do you have for me?" he said, leaning on the table.

I opened the lid. "A purse and its contents."

"It looks vintage," James said, pulling the box closer. He reached for a pair of disposable gloves from his pocket and slipped them on. He picked up the purse, opened it, and peeked inside. "It should be quick."

"Thanks, James," I said. "Were you here in 1997?"

"Yes," he said, frowning. "Is that how old the case is?" He pointed at the box and returned the purse.

"Yes," I said. "And the investigating officer seemed to have closed the case before bothering to do any actual police work."

"Who was the officer?"

I read the one-page statement. "Officer Eugene Aldridge."

James arched eyebrows. "No surprise there. He was the most useless, lazy officer I'd ever worked with."

"How so?" I asked.

"Well, for one, he was always late, had sloppy evidence cataloguing, and never returned phone calls. I was glad he retired long before his time."

"I'm amazed Captain didn't fire him."

"He was conveniently married to Captain's aunt, so I can only assume he turned a blind eye towards the guy," James said, picking up the box.

It explained why Captain never knew about this case or why he didn't fire Eugene. "Thanks, James, it makes sense. Do you know if we can view old employee files?"

James chuckled. "Check with Captain." He raised a shoulder. "But I doubt you'll get anything."

I sighed audibly. He was probably right. It wasn't often we could view other officers' personal files, but this was an exception. This officer did nothing about this homicide case. How many times had this happened?

Captain's ears had to have been burning because he came in behind James. "Men," he said in his deep baritone. We knew he was nearby even when he whispered. "I hear you've taken on that Jane Doe case."

"Yes, sir," I said, standing. "Were you aware of this case Officer Eugene Aldridge had worked on?"

"No, I knew nothing about it, or I would've instructed him to do a better job. I'm sure you're aware he was married to my aunt." I nodded. "They divorced before I told him to retire in 1997 and then he disappeared," he continued. "I heard he had passed away last year from brain cancer."

"I don't suppose I can look at his employee file?"

"Why do you want that?" His brows squashed together,

making them look like a hairy caterpillar. Captain Emory Payne was a one-of-a-kind man; even his name was unusual. At first glance, he reminded me of a soft teddy bear with bushy eyebrows and wild curly hair, but he was the scariest Captain I'd ever worked with. Nobody took a chance with him, yet Eugene did.

"I would like to see if this was the only case he mishandled or if he did it regularly."

"You don't have to see his employee file because he mishandled everything he touched," Captain said. "Eventually, I gave him cases involving theft or break-ins. That's why I'm shocked to find out he worked a homicide case." Red blotches formed on Captain's neck and cheeks, so I thought it best to leave it for now, but I still wanted to see Eugene's file for any alleged allegations against him.

"Who were the officers who worked with him around that time?"

Captain shook his head, deep in thought. "Nobody wanted to, but he did work with Officer Beckett on one case."

"Thank you, sir," I said. I had only met Officer Beckett once. He was retiring soon and had a desk job doing odds and ends or wherever we needed him.

About the Author

Multi-genre author writing twisted endings...

N Gray is a USA Today Bestselling Author who lives in Cape Town, South Africa, with her daughter and adopted cat named Miss Beans.

During the day, she's an analyst and provider profiler for a medical insurance company. At night, she types on her curved keyboard, creating fictional characters some may love and others you want to kill yourself.

She writes in four genres: urban fantasy, thriller, horror, and paranormal romance.

She now writes under Natalie Michaels for her new thrillers and SD Syns for her new horrors.

Acknowledgments

Thank you to Tammy for always being available to proofread my books.

A special thank you to DRS for reviewing the chapters featuring the Dominant.

Lastly, thank you to my readers, old and new, for taking a chance on my books.

You are the reason I write the stories I do. As long as you keep reading, I'll keep writing.

I'm truly humbled by your support and encouragement.